Heather felt

Ross looked at her. still the sudden tr...... ...g in her fingers. Why had he come here, disturbing her new-found peace? Why did he have to look so…male…so confidently at ease and in control? Her heart was thumping erratically in response to his nearness, her temperature rocketing off the scale. Why was she so aware of him? Perhaps the change of scene was having a bigger effect on her than she had bargained for.

When **Joanna Neil** discovered Mills & Boon®, her lifelong addiction to reading crystallised into an exciting new career writing medical romances. Her characters are probably the outcome of her varied lifestyle which includes working as a clerk, typist, nurse and infant teacher. She enjoys dressmaking and cooking at her Leicestershire home. Her family includes a husband, son and daughter, an exuberant yellow Labrador and two slightly crazed cockatiels.

COUNTRY REMEDY

BY

JOANNA NEIL

MILLS & BOON®

For Daniel and Chelsea

First published in Great Britain 1998
Harlequin Mills & Boon Limited,
Eton House, 18-24 Paradise Road, Richmond, Surrey TW9 1SR

© Joanna Neil 1998

ISBN 0 263 81159 X

Set in Times Roman 10½ on 11¼ pt.
03-9809-55180-D

Printed and bound in Norway
by AiT Trondheim AS, Trondheim

CHAPTER ONE

HEATHER pulled in a deep breath and then released it slowly, unclenching her fingers from their stranglehold on the steering-wheel. It had been several hours since her argument with Martyn, but she was still wound up as tight as a steel spring.

How could he have expected her to go along meekly with all his plans? He was trying to organise her life, for heaven's sake, taking over all the once-and-for-all decisions that should have been hers alone.

And where had all this talk of marriage come from? He had dropped that on her right out of the blue, hadn't he? She hadn't been thinking about marriage at all. It hadn't crossed her mind. As if she would ever fall into that trap after her parents' disaster. No. But she might have been talking to the wall for all the difference it made. He didn't seem to want to understand what she was trying to say, and he had treated her as though she wasn't quite herself and needed guidance. Just like her father. She could feel the tension rising in her again, just thinking about it.

Martyn had had it all worked out. 'The new housing development will be central for both of us. It'll only take me fifteen minutes or so to get to your father's factory from there, and the Malvern partnership will be ideal for you.'

'I haven't decided yet whether to accept it,' she'd said, stiffly.

'Why ever not? You can be a GP anywhere. The job's the same wherever you go.'

'Not necessarily. And, anyway, I need time to think

about it…and about us. I'm sorry, Martyn, but I wasn't expecting this. I'm not ready for any of it. I thought we could just be friends.'

'We're more than that, surely? You're just tired, Heather. You've been working so hard lately, but now your contract's come to an end you can take some time out and we can think about being together.'

She'd shaken her head. 'I told you, I've already made up my mind what I want to do—at least for the next few weeks. I'm going to visit my grandfather. It's been such a long time since I last saw him, and I miss him.'

'You can't still be thinking of going… It's a crazy idea to just take off like that…'

He had tried cajoling her at first, and when that hadn't worked he had started to get angry. The scene played itself over in her head and she shivered a little, despite the warmth of the afternoon sunshine. His outburst had touched some inner core, a hidden remnant of the anxious times when she had listened in on her parents' arguments and wished they would end.

Determinedly, she pushed the disturbing thoughts away. The city was behind her now, and she turned the car smoothly into the rutted country lane. She was nearly there—home, at last… The beginnings of a smile touched her mouth. It really felt like that—as though she was coming home, back to where she belonged.

How long had it been since she was last down here? Was it really six months? She shook her head in disbelief. Time had just seemed to have been eaten up lately. There'd been so much to do, with short-staffing and sick leave to be covered, and there had been scant opportunity to get away.

Things had changed now, though. These last few years had been filled with nothing but work, hard, determined slog, so that she could get to where she was now, but it had all been worth it in the end—hadn't it?

She was Dr Heather Brooks, GP. She tested the words
on her tongue, savouring them. The very sound had her
smiling all over again. There was time enough now to
make up her mind about what she wanted to do with her
future. There was the Malvern offer to consider but it
could wait. She wasn't expected to decide straight away.
It would be some months before they needed a definite
answer and for now she simply wanted to put everything
behind her and recharge her batteries.

She needed to spend some time with the old man she
loved most in the world, and she was glad she had made
the break. She couldn't wait to get to the house and see
her grandfather again, to fling her arms around him and
hug him tight. Just the thought of spending time with
him made her heart feel lighter. She had missed him so
much, and seeing him again was all that mattered now.

Glancing around, she saw that the hedgerow was beginning to thin out and give way to a row of familiar
houses made cheerful with brightly coloured hanging
baskets and gardens decked with varying hues of azalea
and rhododendron, scarlet tulips and purple aubrietia.

Heather felt the tension of the last few months slip
from her shoulders as she caught sight of the spreading
oak tree that marked the track leading to her grandfather's house. Set back from the road, the white-painted
cottage was reached by a winding gravel path, bordered
by flowering shrubs and a huge old crab-apple tree, its
branches weighed down with crimson blossom.

Parking the car on the drive, she switched off the engine and stepped out, looking around her appreciatively.
The front wall of the house and the porch were covered
by a rambling japonica, its yellow flowers reflecting the
heat of the sun in a welcome that warmed her heart.
There was the scent of hyacinths on the air, and she
breathed it in deeply as she walked towards the front
door and pushed her key into the lock.

'Grandad…' She called out to him, her blue eyes filled with happy anticipation. She went into the living room and said his name again, glancing quickly around. A moment later the door that gave on to the kitchen was pushed open and she came to a standstill, waiting to see the familiar craggy features.

Only it wasn't her grandfather who came into the room, and her smile wavered a bit as she found herself unexpectedly confronted by a total stranger. He was long-limbed, a vigorously fit-looking man, who strode purposefully across the carpeted floor towards her. She stared at him, nonplussed for a moment.

He stopped abruptly, and his vivid grey-blue glance widened a fraction as he slanted it over her, taking in the cloudy mass of shoulder-length honey blonde curls and the slender shapeliness of her figure in the soft denim dress.

'I thought I heard a car pull up.' The deep voice, rumbling up from his chest, came as a kind of shock to her senses, and caused strange things to happen in the region of her stomach. His glance shifted from her to the framed photo on the mahogany table by the window, and back again. 'You must be Heather.' He paused. 'You're very like your photograph,' he added, his firmly sculpted jaw moving in a wry manner that she couldn't quite fathom.

'You have the advantage of me, I'm afraid,' she told him frankly, studying him in turn, her mood plummeting rapidly from the earlier eager expectation to one of wary curiosity.

His hair was black, crisply styled to frame angular features which would at any other time have rated more than a second glance. He was wearing well-cut grey trousers, she noticed, and his faintly striped shirt was laundered to perfection, the cuffs rolled back to reveal strong, tanned forearms covered with a smattering of dark hair. He was lean and well muscled, so definitely male that she had to quell an odd feeling of breathlessness.

'Kennedy,' he supplied, easily enough. 'Ross Kennedy. Sam told me you were driving down here today.' He looked at her thoughtfully for a moment, then said, 'Come through to the kitchen.' He turned and headed back that way, moving confidently—expecting her to follow. She hesitated for a second or two, then went after him.

'I was just making some tea,' he murmured. 'I expect you're parched after your journey.' It might have been a friendly enough offer, but his tone was coolly matter-of-fact, formally polite. It was a strange feeling, being invited into her own territory by a total stranger. As he spoke he searched the cupboards for crockery, setting things out on a tray before going over to the fridge and taking out a bottle of milk.

Heather tried to gather her scattered wits. His name had drawn a blank in her memory, but he certainly seemed to have the run of the place, as though it was perfectly natural for him to be here. Even so, she knew nothing at all about him. She stirred restlessly. What was going on? She'd come here to see her grandfather, but where was he? She wasn't inclined to stop and take tea with someone she didn't know from Adam—not yet, anyway.

'You're right. I am thirsty,' she admitted, 'but I think I'll forego the drink until I've seen my grandfather. Where is he, do you know?' For all she knew, something might have happened to him.

Perhaps he caught the guarded note in her voice because he shot her a quick look and said evenly, 'I persuaded him to sit in the garden for a while. He's been listening out for you for the last couple of hours, and it

seemed a shame for him to be missing out on the sunshine, especially when he loves the garden so much.'

So he knew her grandfather well enough, then. Maybe
he was a neighbour, someone fairly new to the area. She
relaxed a little.

'I'm later than I meant to be. I had some trouble getting away,' she confided ruefully, remembering Martyn's
last-minute attempts to keep her from leaving, 'and then
I met with a lot of congestion on the roads.'

He made a faint grimace, then said sharply, 'Two
hours isn't going to make much difference after all this
time. He's been looking forward to your visit.'

'So have I.' She frowned slightly. 'I planned to come
over a couple of weeks ago, but I had to cancel.'

'So I gather,' he said tersely. 'Sam was upset. He'd
been marking off the days.'

Her glance shot up to meet his. Was he deliberately
trying to make her feel guilty? It was scarcely her fault
that one of her colleagues had to take compassionate
leave. 'Obviously, I didn't have any choice.'

'Would it have made any difference? You weren't
about to drop everything as soon as you heard that he
was ill, were you?' He shrugged. 'People have different
priorities, of course. Still,' he added briskly, 'now that
you are here at last you might take his tea out to him
while I hunt out some food.' Without ceremony, he
pushed the loaded tray into her hands and went to toss
cookies from a jar on to plate, leaving her to contemplate
the back of his head and the broad sweep of his shoulders with a puzzled frown.

Ill? What exactly had he meant by that? She'd known
about the bronchitis, but it hadn't been serious, by all
accounts. She'd spoken to Sam on the phone yesterday,
and the only mention of any illness had been made under
duress when she'd quizzed him some more about his

wheezy chest. Apart from that, he'd sounded as cheerful as ever.

Ross Kennedy was beginning to annoy her with his offhand manner. She forced herself to take a slow breath. First things first. Her grandfather was outside, he'd said, so she'd go and find him and work out later what this unsettling man was doing here, creating eddies in her new-found pool of peace.

She went out into the garden with the tray, her stiffness fading as she stepped onto the terrace. It was all heart-warmingly familiar out here, the mellowed, sand-coloured paving stones that formed wide circles on the curving expanse of lawn giving way to the herbaceous border and backdrop of ornamental trees. She followed the well-worn path to the little arbour and found her grandfather there, oblivious, sitting on the rustic bench watching the flies disturb the surface of the fish pond.

He hadn't heard her approach. A low stone wall bordered the steps a few feet away, and she placed the tray carefully on the flat coping stone, straightening to look, misty-eyed, at the white-haired old man. The sight of him came as a shock. He looked so frail, much frailer than when she had last seen him, his dear, weather-beaten face thinner somehow.

Her quiet movements must have filtered through to him because he turned slowly, his cheeks creasing into a smile that had her own mouth curving in response. She crossed the few yards of grass between them, put out her arms and hugged him close, her cheek resting against his.

'Oh, I've missed you,' she told him. 'I couldn't bear to let the summer pass without coming to see you.'

'And it's good to see you, girl,' he said gruffly, returning the hug. 'Let me look at you properly.' His grey eyes feasted on her. 'You look fit and well enough—a bit pale, mind, but that's the town for you and I expect you've been working too hard. The country air will soon put come colour back in your cheeks.' He smiled, pulling in a ragged breath of air, as though the little speech had been almost too much for him.

'You're a fine one to talk,' she admonished him, a catch in her voice. 'What have you been doing to yourself?'

'Me? Nothing that a cup of tea won't put right. I was beginning to think I was sitting in a desert.' He sketched a meaningful glance towards the teapot and she hid her concern behind a grin and went to pour.

'How's the chest?' she asked a moment later when he had his drink to hand and she was sitting beside him.

'It'll do. Can't expect miracles at my age.' He glanced across the lawn. 'Ah, Ross, there you are, lad, and you've made sandwiches. Good. Give some to Heather. She must be hungry after coming all this way.'

The 'lad' must be all of thirty-four, thirty-five, Heather thought, stifling a smile. Ross obliged with the sandwiches, passing another plate to Sam and saying firmly, but with an oddly gentle note, 'Try to eat something yourself, Sam. You're all skin and bone, and it won't do. You need building up a bit. Maybe now that your granddaughter's here she'll keep you in line.' He helped himself to tea as Sam wafted a shaky hand dismissively in the air.

'She's here for a visit, not to fetch and carry and fuss about.'

Heather shook her head at that. 'Ross has a point, you know. You're obviously not well, Grandad, and you clearly need taking in hand. Perhaps I ought to have a word with your doctor and see if between us we can get you on the mend?'

'Ross is taking care of all that, don't you fret, love.' Heather eyed him questioningly and he added, 'He's the local doc. I never thought I'd come to need one, but he's a good man, even if he does get a bit stroppy now and then. Insists I have regular check-ups. Forever taking my blood pressure and listening to the old chest. Likes his own way, you know.' He paused for breath and chuckled. 'A bit like your father,' he added with a touch of mischief. 'Always thinks he knows best.'

'You should do as you're told, you old reprobate,' Ross put in drily. 'And it's time you learned your limitations, too. Let Heather help where she can. You've been warned—the old heart's not as strong as it was and you need to accept help where it's offered, not struggle with everything on your own as before.'

Heart? Heather frowned, studying Sam keenly. She had been shocked to see him looking so ill, and perhaps that was the explanation. 'We're not talking about bronchitis, at all, are we? What's going on? What have you been keeping from me?'

Ross flashed her a glance. 'You didn't know?'

Heather swallowed hard. 'I didn't know.'

He sent her a frankly sceptical look then turned to Sam, his dark brows drawing together. 'You said you'd told her. What, exactly, did you say?'

The old man shifted uncomfortably. 'Heather has her own life to lead. She'd only have dropped everything and rushed down here, and for what? You're doing everything that's necessary. She couldn't have done any more.'

'She's a doctor, isn't she? I'm sure she could have done a good deal.'

Heather looked from one to the other, then shook her head in growing consternation as she turned her blue gaze back on her grandfather. 'You've had a heart attack, is that it?' she asked, dismayed. Her throat constricted as she saw the truth written in his rueful expression. 'And I knew nothing...' Her voice trailed bleakly away.

'I didn't want you worrying, girl, and Ross came by when it happened. He shipped me off to hospital and took care of everything, then and now. Even had the house ready for me when I came home.'

'Which was…when?' She directed the question at Ross.

'A few weeks ago,' he supplied. 'He spent some time in the coronary care unit. Which reminds me…' He glanced at his watch. 'I should be on my way. I want to call in at the hospital to check on some test results—a biopsy I did a day or so ago on a patient with a suspect mole. A friend of mine works in the lab there, and said he would try to hurry things up a bit. It's one thing to do minor surgical procedures at the practice for the convenience of the patient, but the follow up still takes time.'

He quickly swallowed the last of his tea, his throat moving in a way that momentarily distracted her. Then he put his cup down and stood up. 'I'll leave you to catch up on things with Heather,' he said, addressing Sam. 'You take care…' He nodded to Heather, before starting to move off across the lawn.

She stared after him. He was going, when there was so much more she needed to know. She scrambled to her feet and glanced quickly at her grandfather, but he waved her off and she hurried after Ross.

He'd moved faster than she'd expected, taking the path that went around the side of the house. He had almost reached the front drive before she succeeded in catching up with him.

She touched his arm briefly, but long enough for her fingers to register the warmth of his skin through his shirtsleeve and tingle as though she'd made contact with a bolt of electricity.

He stopped and turned to look at her, and she was

conscious once more of his height and of a quiet strength
in the long, lean body, held in check.

'I'd like a quick word before you go.' He waited, and
she went on, 'I should thank you for taking care of my
grandfather. I'd no idea what had happened—I still have
no real idea. Was it an MI?'

Ross nodded, and her spirits sank. Myocardial infarc-
tion was the thing that had come first to her mind. 'How
serious is it?'

'Bad, I'm afraid. I came by here purely by chance that
day and I was able to treat him there and then, but the
damage had already been done. The blood tests afterwards showed high enzyme levels so the outlook isn't
good.'

He had been brutally candid and Heather absorbed the
information with a growing sense of shock, but pulled
herself together enough to ask, 'And the treatment now?'

'Beta-blockers to reduce the demand on his heart. He
insisted on coming home, against our wishes. The neighbours have been keeping an eye on him and the district
nurse has been calling on a regular basis.'

'You, too?'

'Of course.'

Heather swallowed against the lump in her throat. 'I
can't thank you enough for all you've done. Now that
I'm here I'll see to it that he's looked after. You won't
need to worry any longer.'

'That remains to be seen, doesn't it?' he remarked
with a rasp, clearly unconvinced. 'But at least he'll have
someone close by for a while. How long are you planning on staying around? A couple of weeks? This isn't
your area, is it? I expect you'll have to get back shortly,
won't you?' His tone was curt, vaguely dismissive, and
she had the strong feeling he was still critical of her. No
matter what she did or said, she wasn't going to change

his opinion of her. She shrugged the thought to one side. She didn't need his approval.

'Didn't he tell you? I've taken on some temporary work down here to give me the chance to stay on for a couple of months. I'll be based at the hospital. It's night work, three nights a week, covering for the GPs in the area, so I can be with him in the daytime. I'll have to make provision for him at night, of course, but I'll think of something. At any rate, you won't need to feel that you have to be quite so involved as you have been up to now.'

He sent her a cool look. 'That's as maybe. I'll continue to visit as usual—he is still my patient, after all, and, besides, I look on him as a friend as much as anything. As to the rest, we'll see how it works out.'

Heather bit her lip. Despite her attempt to be unconcerned by his manner, his distant tone jarred. She'd always thought of herself as a warm, caring person, and to have him dismiss her so easily was unexpectedly hurtful. To be fair, though, he did have her grandfather's interests at heart, and he wasn't leaving anything to chance.

'From all that I've heard so far, you must have been a very good friend to him.'

His mouth moved briefly in what might have been a smile but was more likely a grimace. 'His friends have all stood by him when he needed them.'

Again she felt the guilt wash over her, but she braced herself. His attitude had been frosty all along, but she wasn't going to let him get to her.

'I really have to go,' he said. 'If the test result is positive I want to move quickly to give my patient the best chance of recovery.' Then he walked briskly away in the direction of the street, leaving her alone on the drive.

Presumably his car was the sleek, roomy model she

could see parked at the kerbside. She didn't stay to watch him go. Dr Ross Kennedy had left her feeling decidedly rattled, and she would do her very best to put him out of her mind.

CHAPTER TWO

HEATHER went back to Sam in the garden and sat next to him on the bench, where they watched the fish swim lazily in the pond. It was peaceful here, with only the faint rustle of leaves, disturbed by the light breeze, and the sound of birdsong on the air.

'It's good to be back,' she said, laying her hand warmly over his. 'Just you and me and this little quiet place in the middle of all the rush and hassle of the world.'

He chuckled. 'I remember times when it wasn't so quiet. When you and your brother ran about the place, creating mayhem, and your mother and grandmother had their hands full to keep track of you, God bless them.'

They were both quiet then, thinking of the two who were no longer with them. Heather thought wistfully of the times she and James had spent here with their grandparents, not exactly as a complete family since their father hadn't been with them, but there had always been love and laughter. That was what she remembered most. It was so different from her life at home.

Her grandfather broke the silence, asking, 'And how are things back home? Is that fellow you've been seeing still working for your father? Martyn, isn't it? Being groomed for stardom, is he?'

She nodded. 'Dad thinks a lot of him. More than he does of James, I sometimes think, which seems a shame, considering how much time and effort James puts in.'

'Ah, but James is family, and family are expected to give their all, aren't they? At least, I expect that's how your father sees it.'

'You're probably right.' She sighed, thinking about her brother. He had always tried so hard to please their father. They both did, but sometimes it seemed they were attempting the impossible. Robert Brooks had a domineering personality, always needing to be in control, and the business always had to come first. Even to the extent that her mother's yearning for a career had had to be squashed. Had it been worth it in the end, for either of them? Was it any wonder she herself wanted to steer clear of marriage and keep her independence?

Sam had paused to take a breath. Now he said, 'Are you and Martyn serious about each other, then? Are you thinking of tying the knot?'

Her shoulders lifted. 'Martyn wants to.'

He sent her a thoughtful glance. 'You've been going around together for some time, haven't you? What is it now, a couple of years?'

'About that, I suppose. I can't quite remember when it all started. He seems to have been around for a long time now. First he used to come to the house a lot to see Dad on business, and we sort of finished up having the odd meal together. After a while he seemed to be around most of the time. It was comfortable, I suppose. People were so used to seeing us together that we became a pair.'

'But you're not sure about him?'

She grimaced faintly. 'I need more time to think things through.'

Sam shook his head. 'If that's how you feel after all this time, then he's the wrong man for you, girl. You need someone with a bit of spark, a fire to set you alight.'

Heather laughed at that, shaking her head in protest. 'Martyn's a good man. It's just that…I don't know what I want right now. After the way Mum and Dad went on I'm not convinced marriage is a good idea at any time, even with a man who seems to be right.' She made an effort to conjure up Martyn's features, and the fair hair and alert green eyes swam into her mind, but there was no accompanying strength of feeling. She sighed.

'Perhaps I've spent too much time working to get where I am. I've concentrated so hard on getting my qualifications that everything else seems to have taken second place. I've been too busy, and what I really need to do is to stand back a bit and take a look at where I'm headed.'

His brows drew together. 'You don't regret taking up medicine?'

'Never!' She shook her head at that.

'Well, then, might it be working in the city that troubles you?'

'I'm not sure,' she confessed. 'I'm a bit muddled right now. I don't seem able to figure out exactly which bit is bothering me—Martyn, marriage, city life or the thought of living in Dad's shadow.'

'Perhaps it's the whole package,' Sam ventured. 'At least here you'll be removed from all that for a while. Country life might give you a new perspective on things.' He smiled. 'Ross has lived around here for a number of years now, and he wouldn't dream of going back to the city. Life goes at a different pace here, he reckons. The problems are still there, the pressures are the same at times, but at the end of the day you get to know the community better than you would in a big city practice. It's the people that matter, above all else.'

'I'm glad you've had him around to look after you,' Heather said, smiling. No matter what personal reservations she might have about Dr Kennedy and his cool, somewhat abrupt manner, at least he had been good to her grandfather. 'You two get on well together, don't you?'

'We do. He's well liked around here. Perhaps you'll

get to know him a bit better if you're staying on for a while. You could even end up as friends.'

She winced inwardly. For her grandad's sake, she would do her best to get along with the man but, given that he wouldn't even trust her to look after her own family, it wasn't likely that she could ever take to him.

'Maybe,' she murmured. 'So, let's talk about what we plan to do together these next few months. I've got the car so I can take you out and about if you like…when you're feeling more up to it…and there's the garden, of course. I'll potter about in it, but you'll have to tell me if there's anything that needs doing first of all.'

He patted her hand contentedly. 'You're an angel, just like your mother. It's good to have you back, girl.'

Heather's work as a locum started a few days later, and she was feeling a bit easier in her mind about it now that she had shown Sam how to page her in case of an emergency.

'There won't be any call for that,' he argued. 'I don't want you to have to be worrying yourself and, anyway, Ross phones or visits most days to check up on me.' But she'd stuck to her guns and made sure he knew what to do.

'I know he does, but you're my grandad and I love you. Any problem at all, and I'll come home.' She glanced at the clock and hesitated, still a little anxious about leaving him, but relief washed over her as his friend arrived on time to sit with him for the evening. She started out for the hospital in a better frame of mind, knowing that the arrangements she'd made were reasonably secure.

She only hoped this new job would work out as she'd planned. All the discussions had been carried out over the phone with a Dr Manning, who was to be her colleague. She'd no idea what he was like, except that he had sounded friendly enough, though harassed through overwork and relieved that she was going to help out.

The hospital was a rambling old building but the receptionist pointed her in the direction of the wing where the overnight surgeries would be held, and she headed over there, a brisk determination coming into her step.

'Dr Brooks?'

She vaguely recognised the voice. A young man in a dark suit reached for the swing doors and pushed them open for her as she was about to enter. She glanced at him, smiling.

'Thanks. Yes, I'm Heather Brooks.' He had a pleasant face and an open and friendly expression.

'I'm Jim Manning. We spoke on the phone. Glad to have you join us,' he said, putting out a hand and ushering her into an office off the corridor. 'Coffee first, I think,' he murmured, going over to the filter machine set up on a worktop at the side of the room. 'Then I'll show you around the place and help you find your feet— while we have the chance.' He grinned.

'Things might get busy later. This is a fairly new scheme we're trying out—relieving the local GPs overnight—but people are getting used to it and we tend to get more of them dropping in than we did at first.' He pulled a chair out for her and went to take a seat opposite.

'As I explained before, one of us stays here to deal with people who walk in to the centre, while the other goes out on calls.' He sent her a slightly worried look. 'Are you still OK about doing the off-base bit tonight? I'm not sure how familiar you are with the area.'

'I'll be fine,' she told him. 'I know my way about, more or less, and it shouldn't take me long to get my bearings.'

'That's good. When you've finished your coffee I'll show you the consulting rooms. The computers are set up in there so you'll be able to keep a record of patients seen, but we'll need to liaise with the GPs, of course.'

Heather swallowed the remains of her drink and went with him to look over the rooms. Then, after a while, he left her alone to acquaint herself with the filing system and the supplies on hand.

As it turned out, the calls were fairly routine, a suspected heart attack that turned out to be a bad case of dyspepsia and a young woman with a viral infection that had caused a swift rise in temperature and some delirium.

Around eleven, though, she took a phone call from a woman who sounded very distressed.

'I don't know what to do, Doctor. Jessica, my little girl, she's not breathing right. She's making terrible sounds and I'm scared something awful's going to happen to her.'

It took Heather some minutes to calm the mother enough to take down the details. 'How old is your daughter, Mrs Rawlings?'

'She's just two—it was her birthday last week. She didn't seem right then and now it looks as though she's worse. Will you come out right away?'

'Of course,' Heather reassured her. 'You say she wasn't well—can you tell me what seemed to be the problem?'

'It was some sort of infection, I think. Her throat was sore and she had a bit of a cough. Now every time she coughs she makes this awful noise, and I'm so frightened.'

'Try to stay calm,' Heather said soothingly. 'I'm on my way now.'

Both parents were in an agitated state when Heather arrived at the house, and the little girl, who was clinging to her mother, seemed to have picked up on this. She was fretful and hot, her cheeks streaked with salty tears and her fair hair curling damply about her head. Mrs Rawlings was pacing the room with her while her husband looked on worriedly.

'Why don't you sit down with her for a while, Mrs Rawlings?' Heather suggested. 'You both look worn out.' She sat down on the settee beside them and listened to the characteristic noise the little girl made as she struggled for breath. Gently she stroked the child's hair. It sounded as though the larynx was inflamed and possibly obstructed, and that could be serious. 'There, sweetheart. We'll soon make you better. Poor little love. Shall I have a look and see what's the matter?'

After a while Jessica relaxed a little, her sobs subsiding. She rested her head against her mother, allowing Heather to run the stethoscope over her chest and examine her throat. The little girl's breathing was certainly difficult and noisy when she was upset, but it did seem to ease a bit when Heather gently reassured her.

'That's fine, chick. Your throat's very sore, isn't it? That's been upsetting you and making your cough worse. We'll see what we can do to make you feel a bit more comfortable.'

Turning to the mother, she said quietly, 'I think she has croup. The inflammation in the throat is causing some stickiness to collect there, and every now and again the larynx goes into a spasm, which adds to her distress. It would help if we could sit with her in a warm, steamy atmosphere—running a bath would be ideal.'

'I'll go and run one now.' Dave Rawlings was obviously glad to be able to do something useful, and he shot off to the bathroom straight away. Taking her cue from Heather, his wife lifted the little girl in her arms and carried her upstairs, sitting with her on a stool at the side of the bath and doing her best to comfort her.

'Keep the steam going for about a quarter of an hour and she should soon be feeling a lot better,' Heather advised. Dave waited with them until Jessica had settled in her mother's arms, and then he went downstairs to make tea.

Heather watched the child carefully, listening to the changing note of her breathing. After a time said, 'She's beginning to settle down nicely, isn't she? I'll give her a sedative, and she'll probably sleep for a few hours. You can repeat the process with the steam whenever you like over the next few days.'

She stayed with the parents for another half-hour or so until the little girl was fast asleep and tucked up in bed. Their relief that the panic was over was plain to see, and she didn't think they would have any trouble handling any future episodes.

'I think she'll be fine now but give me a ring if you're at all concerned.'

She went out to her car and started the drive back to the hospital to give Jim Manning a hand. Her mobile phone sounded just as she was turning into the car park and she cut the engine to take the call.

'Martyn...You took me by surprise. I thought it was a patient ringing me.'

'You're going ahead with the job, then?'

'Of course.'

He tutted irritably. 'When am I going to see you? Are you coming home at the weekend or on your days off?'

'I can't.' Quickly, she told him about Grandad's illness. 'I have to stay here to take care of him. He needs me.'

'Aren't you being over-protective? There are organisations, people, to take care of things like that.'

'How can you even suggest it? He's my grandad. I want to stay and look after him myself, at least until he's on his feet again.'

'And what about me? Don't my feelings count for

anything? You just took off, when you knew we had so much to talk about.'

Heather made an effort to appease him. 'Try to understand, Martyn. I have to do this. I need to know that he's all right.'

'No, I don't understand,' he said curtly. 'You don't have to stay there, you're choosing to. You have a life here, Heather, a job waiting for you…'

She heard his voice, but the words were drowned out by the drumming that started up in her ears. He was bullying her, trying to get her to go along with his wishes, just as her father had always done. Tension gripped her stomach, and a sick feeling rose in her.

He was trying to make her feel guilty, and suddenly she was swamped by all the feelings she'd had as a child when she had listened to her parents arguing. It was that same feeling of uncertainty about what was happening, the feeling that somehow she was to blame. But how could she have been? And why was she letting him get to her now, letting him put her through the familiar misery?

'I'm not coming back, Martyn,' she said. 'Not until I'm ready. There's nothing to stop you from coming over here, though. You know where to find me.'

'And you know that isn't easy right now,' he retorted. 'Your father's in the middle of reorganising the company. This is a busy time.'

'For me, too. I have to go now, Martyn. I'm supposed to be working. We'll talk some other time when you're calmer.'

She cut the call and sat quietly for a moment or two to settle her frazzled nerves. Then she got out of the car and walked towards the hospital.

It was fairly quiet at this time of night, and everything was cloaked in darkness so she was glad of the security lights as she walked up to the building.

A man was coming out of the main doors, his step firm and decisive, and perhaps it was that, as much as the sight of his somehow familiar, long, lean frame, that made her give him a second glance. He was a man who knew where he was going, someone who was very confident, very sure of himself. The shadows lent an added authority to his features.

'Dr Kennedy.' It was strange, bumping into him at this time of the night, and perhaps she sounded as tense as she was feeling because he stopped and gave her a searching look.

'Dr Brooks. Is everything all right?'

'Fine, thanks,' she said stiffly. 'It's just that this is the last place I expected to see you. I didn't think you would be working this late in the evening now that we have this new system in operation.'

'I'm not. I came to visit a patient—a friend. He's just gone through surgery on his knee—a synovectomy. He was depressed because someone told him the effects of the operation might not last.'

'An arthritic? Isn't he on medication? That should prevent any return of the symptoms once the synovial membrane has been removed.'

'That's what I told him. He won't be jumping around for a while, but eventually his mobility will improve.'

'How did your biopsy patient fare?' she asked.

'It was positive, unfortunately, but I managed to get him an urgent appointment. I'm reasonably confident we caught it in time.'

'Let's hope so.' She glanced towards the main door. Perhaps it was the aftermath of her conversation with Martyn, but she felt that she needed to get away now, be on her own. 'Well...I'd better look in on my base and check on things.'

He didn't seem to be in any hurry to move, though. 'Is this your first night on call?'

'That's right.'

'How are things going?'

'Well enough.'

His glance narrowed on her. 'If you need any help with anything, you've only to say.'

She frowned. Did he think she couldn't cope? 'That won't be necessary,' she answered in a level tone. 'I can manage perfectly well.'

'I'm glad to hear it. Did you manage to sort out your arrangements with Sam?'

'Of course. He'll page me if there's a problem. I told you there was no reason for you to be concerned.'

Ross's mouth twisted. 'I was just asking. I had it in mind to keep him company for the odd evening, as I have done in the past, but I don't want to tread on your toes.'

A faint flush of heat ran along her cheeks, and she hoped he wouldn't notice in the semi-darkness. 'I'm sure he'd like that. Don't mind me. If you feel like spending an evening with him anytime, go ahead. He needs male company.'

'I'll bear it in mind.' As Heather made to move away from him, he glanced down at her medical bag and said with a frown, 'Are any of my patients on your list?'

The question rattled her. Did he feel he needed to check? 'None so far. But there's no need for you to worry—I'll keep you informed. I'll do my best to see that they come to no harm.'

His eyes glittered at that. 'I only meant that if you come up against any problems I might be able to throw some light on the situation.'

'That's thoughtful of you, but I'm sure I shall cope.' She gave him what might have passed for a smile and said, 'You'll have to excuse me. I should get back to work.'

His eyes narrowed, but he let her go, without saying

anything more. She was conscious, though, of his gaze fixed on her as she made her way into the building. What was it about the man that made her skin tingle and set her nerves on edge?

She made a determined effort not to think about him, but to concentrate her whole mind on her job.

Things were more or less quiet for the rest of the night, until her last call came around six in the morning.

Richard Stanway was a young man who was apparently suffering a lot of pain. It was mostly in his back, he had told her over the phone, and it had woken him in the early hours. She had to wait a while for him to open the door to her and she guessed it must have been a struggle for him to manage the stairs. He was about twenty years old, she judged, and she guessed he was living alone in the rented flat.

She frowned, watching his stiff movements. He was lean, verging on thin, and she wondered if he was looking after himself properly.

'I'm sorry I had to call you out,' he apologised, 'but I didn't think I could cope without something for the pain. When I rang you I wasn't even sure I could get out of bed. The paracetamol I took doesn't seem to be having any effect, and I have to be fit for work later this morning.'

'What work do you do?' she asked.

'I help out on a farm just a couple of miles away. I can't not go in,' he explained. 'They're short-handed as it is, and the animals have to be fed. I only started the job a week or so ago, and I don't want to risk losing it. The way I feel at the moment, though, I doubt if I could get out of the house.'

Heather could understand how he felt, especially if he was fending for himself. She wondered about his family, but kept quiet for the time being and concentrated on finding out what was wrong with his back.

'Have you fallen or jarred your spine in any way?' she asked as she carefully examined him. There was a marked degree of stiffness that worried her, and she thought that he must have been suffering for quite some time. Instinct told her there might be the possibility of disease.

'Not that I recall. I've had trouble with it for a few months now—the mornings are the worst, especially the early hours like now. Then it wears off a bit during the day. Not getting a decent night's sleep doesn't help. People think I've been out, living it up, when I'm dozy around lunchtime.'

She hid a wince as his comments added to her suspicion that this was more serious than some vague injury. Instead, she nodded in sympathy. 'Doesn't seem fair, does it?' she said with a wry smile. 'You can get dressed now, Richard. Who is your doctor?'

Richard pulled on his shirt. 'I think it's the one at the crossroads. I only moved into the area a few weeks ago so I haven't been into the surgery. It's the big house with ivy over the walls.'

'I know the one you mean.' She frowned. From the quick study she'd made of the area covered by the locum team, she realised that it must be Ross Kennedy's practice, about a mile down the road from her grandfather's place. From the size of the house, there was probably family accommodation included, and she wondered if he was married or had any children. It occurred to Heather that she might find herself dealing with Ross and his patients rather more than she had expected, and she wasn't quite sure how she felt about that, given his initial antipathy towards her.

Her shoulders straightened. She was a professional, wasn't she? She'd dealt with difficult people before. Just because this time it was somehow more personal shouldn't make any difference.

'I think you'll need to go to Outpatients at the hospital so that they can do some tests,' she told Richard, dragging her thoughts back to the present. 'I suspect that there's some inflammation in your spine. I can give you some tablets to help in the meantime, but we need to know more about what's going on. I can make the arrangements for an appointment, but I'll need to let your GP know what's happening. Do you have any family who can give you a bit of support until you're feeling better?'

He shook his head. 'I came here to get away from them. Well, from my dad, anyway,' he added with a touch of bitterness. 'We were always arguing. I could never do anything right by him. We've not very much in common—he's into sport, always on at me to play matches and so on, but I'm just not good at that kind of thing. So in the end I decided to get out and have some kind of independence.'

'Do they live far away?'

'Lower Huxbridge. About ten miles from here. But I don't need them, not if you can fix me up with some pills. My dad will just think I'm putting it on, and my mum will only worry.'

His answer saddened her. She sensed that behind the bravado there was disillusion and unhappiness. It was always painful when families broke up—there was always a sense of frustration, of lives disrupted. She had been through it herself, hadn't she?

'The tablets should help to ease the pain, but you could do some gentle exercises each day to keep the spine supple once the pain wears off. I'll give you an exercise sheet.'

'OK, whatever you say. Thanks, Doctor.'

She wrote a prescription and searched in her medical bag for a couple of tablets to tide him over until he could get to the chemist. Then she let herself out, pulling the collar of her jacket around her to ward off the early morning chill. It was still quite dark, the sky forbidding and overcast as she drove home, yawning a little and thinking longingly of her bed and the chance to catch up on some sleep. Sam usually went to bed late, and slept in a bit, so hopefully things would work out. Had he been all right? There had been no word from him...

Parking the car on the drive in front of the cottage, Heather stepped out wearily onto the gravel. Perhaps tiredness was affecting her more than she'd realised because a strange noise made her jump and caused her heart to beat out of time. She turned just as a black form sprang towards her out of the gloom. She flattened herself against the metal bodywork of the car, panic rising in her throat.

'What on earth—?' Memories of another time came flooding back, a time when there had been bared fangs and glittering eyes and tearing aggression.

'Toby—come back here! Sit!'

She recognised that deep voice, and the hammering of her pulse subsided to an erratic thud as Ross Kennedy came towards her.

'Are you OK?' He searched her face keenly. 'You look as pale as death—he didn't mean any harm. He's just a bit over-friendly. I'm sorry if he frightened you.'

She stared down at the sleek black Labrador who had settled down by Ross's feet, and tried to gain control of her breathing once more.

'I wasn't expecting anyone—anything—to be around at this time of the morning.' Her voice sounded strained to her own ears. He probably thought she was a nervous wreck, on top of any other doubts he had about her, but she couldn't help the sudden recall of that other time, so long ago, when she had come face to face with the threat of danger. Even now, the thought of it brought damp pearls of sweat to her forehead and made her palms clammy.

He spoke again, tugging her mind back to the present. 'I often walk with him along this way first thing in the morning. Sometimes he comes with me when I call in on Sam, and I suppose that's why he came dashing up to the house.' He was still watching her and frowning, a look of concern in his grey eyes. 'He really won't hurt you, believe me.' She didn't move, and he said gently, 'Heather?' His hands came up and circled her arms, his long fingers curving about her, supportive and strong, and warmth shot through her, causing her pulse to race all over again.

'It was silly of me to react like that,' she muttered unsteadily.

He shook his head. 'You had a shock. Let me help you into the house,' he said, his voice coaxing and deep, smoothing over her rattled senses like warm honey.

'There's no need.' Heather sucked in a lungful of air and made an effort to compose herself. 'I can manage,' she said huskily, shifting away from his distracting hold on her. His eyes narrowed a fraction, but she stiffened her shoulders. He already thought badly of her and she didn't want him thinking she was the sort of woman who went to pieces at the slightest thing.

She glanced down at the dog, Toby, who was staring at her eagerly with his mouth open, panting, as if he'd enjoyed the morning's exercise and was ready for more. Then she turned her gaze back to Ross. 'You took me by surprise, that was all. I'll let you get on with your walk.' Her tone was probably cooler than she had intended, but coming face to face with the dog was beginning to take its toll on her. She was tired after the night's work, and more than a little wound up.

His dark brows met in a frown. 'Well, if you're sure... I should be starting back now if I'm to be ready for morning surgery. There's bound to be a stack of post to go through first. I'll be by again later today to see Sam.' He lingered a moment, but then he called the dog and turned away, heading back along the drive.

Heather stood for a while and watched them go, an odd tremor of unease rippling through her. She'd come here looking for peace and tranquillity, among other things, but somehow she doubted she was going to get them. Not with Ross Kennedy turning up on the scene when she least expected him. Maybe she'd make a point of being out when he called again.

It was only after he'd disappeared from view and she'd let herself into the house that she remembered she should have taken the opportunity to tell him about Richard Stanway. A sigh escaped her. It might have been simple enough to drop a note off at the surgery, but she really ought to talk to him about Richard's case...

Now she would have to see him again, and fairly soon at that. Her teeth gritted. The very thought was unsettling. Why did he have to go and disrupt her way of thinking every time he was near?

CHAPTER THREE

IT MUST have rained while she was asleep because when Heather woke and flung open her bedroom window there was a freshness about everything that had her breathing deeply of the country air. She watched as a dove settled in the branches of the apple tree, calling softly to its mate, and in the distance she could hear the lambs in the fields. A contented smile curved her mouth. She could be happy here.

'It's warming up nicely outside,' she told Grandad, going into his room a few minutes later. 'I've brought you some tea and your tablets.' She put the tray down on his bedside table.

He looked pale today and he was coughing chestily, which made him struggle for breath, and that worried her, but he recovered with a smile as she plumped up his pillows and helped him to sit up.

'Thanks.'

'Do you want breakfast up here? Or perhaps that should be brunch—breakfast and lunch. Toast and cereal, and maybe some grilled bacon and tomato?'

'Sounds good, love. But I think I'll come down in a bit.'

'OK. Let me know when you're ready, and I'll help you to the bathroom.'

A quick go at the housework was called for, she decided, pushing clothes into the washing machine, and then a stint at tidying up the garden. She was dressed for it, anyway, with her most comfortable, snug-fitting jeans and a cotton T-shirt, and her hair knotted up on top of her head out of the way.

'Would you like to sit outside with your paper?' she asked Sam later, when the sun had chased away the last trace of the morning's shower. 'You can tell me what needs doing out there.'

He chuckled. 'Are you sure you know what you're letting yourself in for? There's the May fair coming up, you know, and all the bedding plants to be got ready. Some need pricking out, some will have to be transplanted and the rest ought to be brought out of the greenhouse to harden them off.' He stopped for breath, then added, 'If we could put some on the garden table near my chair, I'll give you a hand.'

'And leave me with nothing to do? You're forgetting, I know you too well,' she admonished, with a glint in her eyes. 'Read your paper and relax.'

She tackled the weeds in the flowerbeds first, before dragging the old table into the shade and starting work on the plants. They talked companionably for a while about this and that until she noticed that he was dozing off in the warmth of the sun, and then she absorbed herself in the task in hand.

So engrossed was she that she almost jumped when a long shadow fell across the table. She glanced around and saw Ross standing there, sunlight dappling his features with gold.

He must have come around the side of the house. For a moment Heather was stunned, taken aback by the sight of him, fit and lean, his long body a perfectly honed example of heart-stopping masculinity.

'You've been busy.' He scanned the plants and then made a quick study of her, his glance shifting down over her slender but well-rounded shape, following the line of denim that moulded the curve of her hips. A glitter of interest sparked in his eyes, and she felt her face heat up. 'What are these—fuchsias?'

His hand brushed hers as they both reached for the

pots at the same time, and she drew back as though she'd been stung, warmth rippling through her veins.

Ross looked at her thoughtfully, and she tried to still the sudden trembling in her fingers. Why had he come here, disturbing her new-found peace? Why did he have to look so…male…so confidently at ease and in control? Her heart was thumping erratically in response to his nearness, her temperature rocketing off the scale. Why was she so aware of him? Perhaps the change of scene was having a bigger effect on her than she had bargained for.

'He's going to sell them at the May Fair,' she managed in an even tone. 'It's all in aid of local charities— the hospital, for one. He was getting a bit anxious about them.'

Ross studied her. 'He'll be glad of your help. I was going to offer to do it myself, but it looks as though you beat me to it.'

'I like the chance to be in the garden. I miss it.' She knuckled back a stray tendril of hair which had escaped the knot, conscious all at once of her grimy fingers. What a sight she must look.

'Are these the last?' Ross inspected the tray full of plants, waiting to be potted. 'I'll give you a hand—I expect you could do with a break.'

'If you like.' He was treating her in a perfectly normal manner and she did her best to respond in a similar way.

'I know I could do with the change and the fresh air,' he remarked, shrugging off his jacket and draping it over a garden chair. 'It was a busy morning, cooped up in surgery, and then I worked my way through a series of health checks for the well-man clinic.'

'Blood pressure, urine samples, weight?' she murmured. 'Was everything fairly routine?'

'Mostly. Except for one man who needs referring to

hospital for possible prostate problems. A lot of visits to the loo in the night.'

'An operation on the cards, then?'

'Possibly. There are some consultants who prefer to leave things as they are, and keep a weather eye on the patient.'

He separated the plants efficiently, using the dibber to make a hole in the middle of the compost. His hands were strong and capable, the fingers large, but he handled the tender plants with infinite care and she watched in fascination.

He sketched a glance over the lawn and banks of flowerbeds. 'It must be hard for Sam, being laid low when he used to be so active.'

Heather stared wistfully at her grandfather, still sleeping in the comfy lounger. 'He's been retired some time now, of course, but I think you're right.' She began to stack the empty plastic trays inside the greenhouse. 'He and my grandmother used to run a small garden centre. He did most of the landscaping work, and Nan saw to the planting side of things. I don't think he's quite used to the fact that she's gone.'

Ross nodded soberly. 'He talks about her sometimes, almost as though she's still here, and then he remembers. It's very sad.' He was quiet for a moment, then said with a change of mood, 'So, don't you have a garden of your own back home?'

She shook her head. 'I live in a flat so I have to make do with just a window-box. There's not much room for anything—just the one bedroom, a kitchen-diner and a small sitting room. No garden, and definitely no pets.'

'Would you want any?' His gaze trapped hers. 'It was a shock for you this morning, having Toby lunge at you from out of nowhere—but I had the feeling there was more to it than that. That you were afraid of something else, perhaps? Have you had some kind of bad experience?'

He was too perceptive by half. The discovery made her vaguely uneasy because she wasn't sure she wanted to tell anyone about her own vulnerabilities, least of all him. Why hadn't he just accepted her assurances that she was all right? Instead, he was waiting, his dark eyes unwavering, and she guessed he wasn't the kind of man who would let things go.

She sighed. 'I should have been over it a long time ago. It was all my own fault, really.' She sought for a way to explain. 'When I was a small child I went with my brother to play on a demolition site near where we lived. We hadn't exactly been forbidden to go there, but we knew it was the sort of place that was off limits.

'To us it was fun, exploring and climbing, but then some of the wooden structures started to collapse and we ran for cover. I hid in a big concrete pipe until the dust settled, and then I found I couldn't get out again because a dog was guarding the entrance. He appeared out of nowhere. It was scary. He had me cornered, and I felt sort of claustrophobic and panicky—helpless, really.'

Just as she had for a few minutes this morning. She didn't like feeling like that. It was weakness, something she had struggled to overcome for the last twenty years or so. She'd thought she'd been winning the battle but, even in the telling, her bottled-up feelings of helplessness over the whole sorry event and its aftermath had come sweeping over her. Her parents had had their biggest row of all afterwards, and Heather had been left with the guilt, as though she had been to blame for everything.

To cover her embarrassment, she turned her attention back to the plants, pushing wooden label sticks into the soil.

'And the business with Toby brought it all back this morning,' he said flatly. 'I'm sorry.'

His gentle understanding was almost her undoing. 'Don't be.' She straightened up. 'Toby seems a fine dog. I just wasn't alert as I should have been or I wouldn't have reacted the way I did.'

'Even so, he does get a bit exuberant at times, but he wouldn't hurt a fly—well, that's not exactly true—maybe he would if he could ever catch one.'

She laughed, and he studied her, a gleam darting in the grey-blue eyes.

'That's better. It's the first time I've seen you smile.' He paused, then added quietly, 'Perhaps we got off to a bad start.'

'That was hardly my fault,' she retorted briskly. 'You assumed I was neglecting my grandfather.'

'I can see that still rankles.' He shrugged. 'Maybe I was too judgemental. Mostly it was due the fact that I'd been on duty for twenty-four hours, up half the previous night on call, followed by a busy day at work. It tells on you after a while. So, if I was a bit short with you, that could have been the reason.'

She made a grimace. A bit short? Curt, brisk, decidedly cool, were the words she'd have chosen, but she said simply, 'The new system will be a great help to you, then? You must welcome the relief, surely?'

'Of course. How's the job going? Have you found your feet yet?'

'Yes, I think so. I like it... And it works out very well, with the situation as it is here.'

'There is that, I suppose. But I don't believe it's a good idea to have women covering the night shift, especially based in the town. I wouldn't sanction it. There are far too many dangers.'

She lifted a finely arched brow at that. 'Isn't that an archaic view of things?'

'Hardly. You can't get away from the fact that women are more vulnerable than men, and to put them in a situation where they are alone and unprotected in the city late at night is asking for trouble. Still, didn't you say it was only a temporary post?'

'I did, but even if it wasn't I don't see it as a problem.' Ross's attitude annoyed her. Some men didn't seem to recognise a woman's right to equal status with men— they had to be dragged by the heels into the twenty-first century! Wasn't her father the biggest proof of that? He still thought men were the superior sex, that women needed male guidance since they were ruled by their emotions and not their heads.

Heather shook off the disturbing reminder. She wouldn't think about her father. That was one of the pressures she was trying to get away from.

'The man who will be doing the job on a permanent basis isn't available yet,' she added. 'He's finishing off a contract somewhere else so they asked me to fill in.' She paused, then said, 'Talking of the relief work, I came across one of your patients last night—Richard Stanway. You may not know him, he's new to the area. I've arranged for him to see a consultant rheumatologist.'

Ross's face sobered. He was serious now, listening attentively, and she quickly described Richard's symptoms to him.

'It looked very much like ankylosing spondylitis to me, and I think it needs to be confirmed and dealt with quickly before too much damage is done to the rest of his spine.'

He grimaced. 'Is there any family history?'

'I don't know. He isn't living with them. Apparently, he doesn't get on with his father.'

Ross pulled a face. 'We'll just have to wait and see what the hospital tests show. I doubt if X-rays will show changes at this stage, but blood tests should give us the answer.'

He picked up the tools they had been using, scraping off the loose soil and placing them in the box along with the rest. Perhaps it was the sound of metal clinking on metal that disturbed Sam, but he began to stir from his sleep, slowly accustoming himself to his surroundings.

'There you are, Ross,' he mumbled, stretching his limbs a little. 'I wondered if you'd drop by today.'

'I thought I'd better in case you decided to tackle the garden in readiness for the May Fair, but I see Heather has it all covered.' He looked down at his hands and made a face. 'I'll clean up in the kitchen, then take a look at you,' he said. 'Are you coming into the house?'

Sam nodded. 'Maybe we can rustle up some tea and scones.' He turned to Heather with the hopeful look of a hungry pup. 'Didn't I see you baking yesterday?'

'You did,' Heather said with a grin. 'Go in, and let Dr Kennedy examine you. I expect he has other calls to make after this. I'll finish off here and put everything away, then I'll put the kettle on.'

She tidied up, and went into the house. She was searching the cupboards for a pot of strawberry jam when Ross came into the kitchen a while later.

'He's gone to look for a pen so that he can do the crossword,' he said, accepting the cup she pushed across the table towards him.

Frowning, she started to slice scones in half, spreading them with butter. 'How do you think he is?' She offered him a scone and he took a bite.

'Not so good, I'm afraid. His chest sounds bad, and I'm concerned about his breathing problems.'

She winced at the blunt statement, but it was what she thought, too. 'Diuretics?' she suggested. 'They might ease some of the congestion.'

He nodded, helping himself to another scone when she

gestured towards the plate. 'He might benefit from a visit
to the physio department at the hospital two or three days
a week as well. There's only so much we can do medi-
cally, and he isn't getting any younger. You've done a
tremendous amount to lift his spirits, but the chance to
get out and mix with others in his situation might cheer
him even more.'

'You're probably right.' She sighed, still anxious, and
stirred sugar into her tea absently. 'I think the May Fair
might give him a boost as well.'

'I expect it will, and it'll be a good chance for him to
see his friends.' His glance flicked over her. 'Will you
be going with him?'

'Of course. I want to make sure he's all right.
Anyway, I have to be on duty there as medical officer
that day.'

Ross started on another scone and her glance went to
the rapidly diminishing pile and back again to Ross, her
mouth twitching. 'You remind me of my brother. He
doesn't eat so much as demolish food—and he never
seems to put on any weight, either. You must both use
up a terrific amount of energy.'

He paused in mid-bite, then grinned, swallowing the
rest and licking his fingers with a sensuous enjoyment
that made her insides quiver. 'I didn't have time for
lunch—and they *are* good,' he said with satisfaction.
Then he added in an interested tone, 'Are the rest of
your family back home?'

'My father and my brother. James is married, with two
small children—he works in the family business, manu-
facturing laboratory equipment. He's clever, very astute,
but I don't think he gets much chance to sit back on his
laurels—my father can be a hard taskmaster.'

'No mention of your mother...'

Her chest tightened. 'She died when I started medical
school.'

'That must have been bad.' His brows met, a line digging into the otherwise smooth surface of his forehead.

'It was.' Her eyes misted a little. 'You don't ever forget, but it does get a bit easier with time.' She drew in a breath. 'What about you? Do you have any family?'

'Some.' He smiled, and she was struck by the change in his features, mesmerised by the magnetic pull of his dark eyes. 'My parents are both alive and well, but there are no grandparents so I've adopted Sam. I hope you won't mind sharing him?' His laughing glance enticed and invited her, and she swallowed hard and tried to damp down the leaping antics of her heart which had started with his teasing smile. The memory of her parents cast a dark shadow on her thoughts.

'I doubt I have any choice. He's very fond of you.' Perhaps that had come out more flatly than she'd intended because he glanced at her thoughtfully and drank the remains of his tea.

'I'd better go. I've one or two more calls to make before I'm through.' His tone was cool, and maybe that was because she had instinctively thrown up a defensive wall. The barriers were in place once more and, in a way, she was glad of that. She needed to stay in command of herself.

She went with him to the door, and Ross asked, 'Are you on duty this evening?'

Heather nodded. 'In another couple of hours.'

'Enjoy your peace, then, while you can,' he said drily. He went out to his car and she returned to the kitchen to stare absently at the empty cups and plates.

He'd adopted Sam, he'd said, and that meant that he was probably going to be around rather more than she had bargained for. It could make things difficult. She sensed, deep down, that he wasn't unaware of her as a woman, and that he wouldn't mind getting to know her a little better, but she preferred to keep things as they were, on a level plain.

Her life was complicated enough right now, with Martyn putting pressure on her and her father angling for them to tie the knot and cement his business relationship with a prospective son-in-law. Oh, she had no illusions on that score. He was keen to get Martyn on board in a way that would bind him to the firm more solidly than if he stayed a mere employee. It was typical of her father. He had to be in control at all times, and he didn't like to be thwarted. Well, that was unfortunate because she had no intention of knuckling under. She would do what was right for her, and at the moment that meant keeping her mind clear and concentrating on Grandad and her work.

On that front, the evening was not as quiet as Heather might have hoped. There was a steady stream of visitors to the centre, and she worked there alongside Jim until around eleven-thirty when she was called out.

There had been an accident—a fall, from what she could make out—but the girl, Natalie Fraser, who had made the phone call was upset and not very coherent. All Heather could gather was that Kevin, the girl's father, was apparently unconscious.

The Fraser household was another in Ross's area, she noted absently as she drove to the house, a red-brick semi in the most built-up part of the region.

The fraught atmosphere hit her as soon as she stepped over the threshold, the tension so strong that you could feel it all around.

'Come in. He's in the kitchen.' A young woman—Natalie, presumably—of about nineteen or twenty, her long brown hair tied back with a scrunch, let Heather into the house and then stood by, looking ashen and shaken. She was probably the daughter because there was some resemblance to the older woman who showed Heather into the kitchen, where the smell of alcohol lay heavily on the air.

'He hit his head on the cupboard,' Mrs Fraser explained, looking anxiously at her husband who was slumped against the sink unit on the floor.

The woman's hands were trembling, Heather noticed. 'How long has he been like that?' she asked.

'About half an hour. He tries to say something every now and again. I've tried talking to him and I soaked a cloth with cold water and put it on the swelling, but we can't get him to his feet.'

Heather knelt down beside the man and inspected the site of his head injury. It didn't look serious. There was no open wound and the area of swelling wasn't very large. She checked his pupils and his ears, and Mrs Fraser said awkwardly, 'He wasn't breathing right. We didn't know what to do, whether to call an ambulance or what.'

Heather's mouth twisted a little. 'I don't think there's too much to worry about. I think your husband's biggest problem is that he's had too much to drink.'

Kevin Fraser mumbled something, but his speech was very slurred and Heather couldn't make out what he was saying. She almost reeled from the smell of alcohol on his breath.

'The doctor needs to look at you,' his wife told him.

There was blood on the floor, and Heather turned her attention to the jagged gash on his hand.

'Don't need no doctor.' Kevin's arm flailed, swiping the air and just missing Heather's face.

Mrs Fraser put a hand to her mouth in horror. 'I'm sorry about that, Doctor. He can be difficult to handle at times. To be honest, I wasn't expecting you to come here tonight. I thought it would be Dr Kennedy who came. He usually knows how to deal with Kevin.'

'The system changed recently,' Heather explained. 'I'm sure I shall manage.' She would have to, pure and simple, unless she wanted Ross Kennedy to think that she couldn't manage his more rowdy patients, and that was absolutely out of the question.

'Kevin cut himself on a bottle opener,' Mrs Fraser said. 'I told him he'd had enough but he didn't listen. He never listens.'

'Too busy wanting his own way and overruling everyone else,' Natalie put in bitterly.

Heather opened her medical bag. 'You've cut your hand, Kevin,' she said, beginning to clean the wound carefully. 'It will need stitching.' Her touch seemed to rouse him once more.

'Get off me—mauling me—get away.'

'You're bleeding,' Heather told him, keeping a firm hold on her patience. 'I think it needs attention, unless you'd prefer to live with a scar.'

He stared blearily at the cut and tried to focus, grunting in what might have been surprise. 'Get on with it, then.' His arm lashed out again and Heather ducked so that it just missed her by inches. Natalie sucked in a quick breath.

'You nearly hit her.'

Kevin's face contorted, became ugly with anger. 'You still here? Get out. I told you, we don't want you and that brat you're carrying—another mouth to feed.' His good hand bunched into a fist and shot out, punching the air.

'Keep still,' Heather's voice cut in sharply. 'I'm trying to stitch this wound.'

Natalie gasped and drew back, protective hands shielding her abdomen. 'He hates me. He's always hated me.'

'He doesn't mean it, Natalie.' Mrs Fraser's distress

was plain to see, and she put an arm out to the young girl. 'He doesn't know what he's saying.'

Kevin snarled, his teeth clenched, his whole body rigid. 'Go on, get out, slut.'

Heather snipped the final suture and started to gather up her things. She wouldn't be sorry to get out of here.

Natalie stared at her father, her mouth working spasmodically, her eyes glittering with hurt and anger. 'He talks about me,' she said, her voice cracking with a mixture of anguish and distaste. 'And look at him—nothing but a drunken slob.'

Her father made another lunge, but his reflexes were slowed, the violence muted by the alcoholic haze. Natalie backed away, viewing him with disgust.

'I'm going. I shan't stay here.' She swung round and hurried out, slamming the door behind her. Her mother, white-faced, went after her, and Heather got to her feet.

After a few minutes the older woman came back into the room and stared down at her husband. 'Now look what you've done. She's gone. Are you satisfied?' But he wasn't listening. His outburst over, his energy was spent, and his chin had dropped to his chest, his eyes glazing over.

'Let him sleep it off,' Heather said. 'The stitches should come out in seven to ten days, but he can go to his local surgery for that. Dr Kennedy will probably want to take a look at his hand.' If only to satisfy himself that she had done a decent enough job, she thought wryly.

She glanced at the woman, searching her face. 'Will you be all right? Is there anyone you could call?'

Sue shook her head. 'I'll get by. I've stuck by him for nearly twenty-five years, but sometimes I hate him. Dr Kennedy's told him he needs to get help for his drink problem, but it's no use. Sometimes I wish I could just up and leave—walk out.' She pulled in a ragged breath, then struggled to compose herself. 'I'm sorry. You don't want to hear all this. I'll see you out.'

She looked as though she was about at the end of her tether, and at the door Heather said, 'If you need help—support of any kind—even if it's just to talk to someone, you can ring me.' She passed the woman a card with her number. 'Or you could go along to your surgery. I'm sure Dr Kennedy would try to help you if he knows what a strain you're under.'

'Counselling, you mean? We'll see.' Mrs Fraser straightened her back. 'Goodnight, Doctor. Thanks.'

Heather's mouth made a grim twist as she walked to her car, her thoughts as dark as the night sky. Why on earth did people put up with this sort of chaos in their lives? For love? After almost twenty-five years there seemed little enough of that to spare in this family. Perhaps love was an illusion, not real at all.

She slid behind the wheel and started up the engine, driving away with a feeling of relief. At least she wasn't tied down—she could move away from it.

Around the next bend, some half a mile down the road, she saw the lone figure of a girl, trudging along dejectedly with slumped shoulders. Heather slowed the car and wound down the window. 'Natalie?'

The girl glanced her way, her eyes puffy with crying. She dashed the tears away with the back of her hand.

'Can I give you a lift anywhere?' Heather asked. 'Will you be going back home?'

Natalie shook her head. 'No, I'm not going home.'

'Don't you think your father might feel differently when he's sobered up?'

'He won't. Anyway, I've had enough. I'll be better off at my boyfriend's place.'

'OK. Get in, and I'll take you there, if you like.' Heather pushed open the passenger door and Natalie climbed in.

'Thanks. The last bus has gone so I was in for a bit of a walk. It's about two miles away,' she added shakily. 'Is that all right?'

'Of course. But you'll have to show me the way.'

'Keep going on this road. Take a left at the lights.'

'Will it be all right for you to stay there?'

'I think so. We've talked about living together, but the flat's so small and Mick's job isn't very secure at the moment and, anyway, the thought of leaving Mum on her own with Dad stopped me.' She swallowed convulsively, putting a hand to her mouth as though she was going to be sick.

'Are you pregnant?' Heather asked, and the girl nodded.

'Either that, or my insides are well and truly screwed up from all the rows.'

'How far along are you? Do you know? It doesn't show.'

'About six weeks, I reckon. I just did the test today.'

'You'll need to go to the surgery to sort out your antenatal care,' Heather murmured.

'I suppose so. Dr Kennedy will think I'm an idiot for getting myself pregnant when everything in my life's upside down. He thinks I should go to college and plan for the future.'

'You have to make your own decisions,' Heather murmured. It was hardly Ross's place to comment, but she wouldn't be at all surprised if he offered an opinion. He probably had strong views on most matters.

'I'll have to tell Mick,' Natalie said. 'The way Dad talks you'd think we'd planned it, but we didn't. It just happened.'

She fell silent, lost in thought. They reached the turning and Heather asked, 'Where now?'

'A few yards further. Just there, that's the one.' She pointed along the row of narrow, down-at-heel town houses and Heather stopped the car. There was a light on, visible from behind the curtains.

'He's home, then.'

'Football on TV.' Natalie managed a smile, the effect softening her features and transforming her from an ordinary-looking girl to a strikingly pretty young woman. 'You've been really great. Thanks for the lift.'

'You're welcome.' Heather watched the girl go into the house and waited a while in case she came out again, but when all stayed quiet she carefully put the car into gear and drove away.

Another patient for Ross—or should that be two? Did he do the antenatals himself? His was a small practice, she'd heard, so it was quite likely he would do a good proportion of them, and that might not go down too well with some of the pregnant mums who might prefer to see a woman.

Still, he would treat them with sensitivity and respect, she guessed. Somehow she had the feeling that his humour and gentleness were not reserved for Sam alone, but that all his patients would be treated as special. It was only with her that he seemed to clash from time to time.

She wasn't going to let that bother her, though. She had problems enough, and she wasn't going to spend any more time thinking about a man who could well turn out to be as opinionated and hard-headed as her father!

CHAPTER FOUR

'LETTER for you.' Sam dropped the lunchtime post on to the kitchen table, ignoring his own, and studied the writing on the envelope addressed to Heather. 'Boyfriend?' he hazarded, and watched her expression. 'Aren't you going to open it?'

She glanced reluctantly at the envelope. 'Later,' she told him, putting it into her pocket. 'I have to get on if I'm to finish tidying up here and get off to the shops. I want to look for some fence posts—a few of them out back look as though they're rotting fast.'

She guessed who the letter was from, and the conflicting emotions were back again. Perhaps she ought to have written, or phoned, after their last sharp words, but she had been putting it off. Of course, Martyn was at work during the day, and the evenings were busy for her.

'You shouldn't have to deal with that,' Sam said gruffly, bringing her mind back to fence posts. 'I don't usually let things slide, but I didn't get around to fixing them last year, with one thing and another.'

'It's no problem. Have you finished with that plate?'

'What? Oh, yes. Here you are.' He handed it to her and she put it alongside the rest of the crockery in the washing-up bowl. He studied her keenly. 'It is from the boyfriend, isn't it?' He nodded towards her pocket. 'Are you expecting bad news from back home? Is that why you don't want to open it?' He squeezed her hand lightly. 'I know things haven't been easy for you, what with your parents arguing—and the split, when it finally came. Then your poor mother...' He broke off, then added gently, 'You deserve a chance of happiness.'

Was he worrying on her account? She made an effort to appear more cheerful. 'I *am* happy,' she told him brightly, 'now that I'm here with you—even if you are a nosy old thing!' She chuckled and took out the letter. 'You know what curiosity did…' All the same, she ripped open the envelope and scanned the contents.

Martyn was sorry they'd argued. He hadn't meant to cause more friction between them. She nodded to Sam. 'Yes—it's from Martyn. He says he's working hard. Apparently, Dad's pleased with the figures for the last quarter.' She peered at him over the top of the letter. 'The lab equipment business is in fine form, by all accounts. He thinks Dad will give him a rise at the end of the month.'

Sam's brows went up at that. There was more in similar vein, and then he'd written, 'Missing you. Come home soon, Heather, I want you back here, with me.'

She didn't read that bit out, but pondered his words soberly and wondered why she didn't feel anything. She ought to feel something, didn't she, if their relationship had anything going for it? She glanced up and saw that Sam was looking at her, his kind face creased in a frown.

'Not much there to ask how you're doing,' he muttered. 'No wonder you're not sure of yourself.'

She smiled faintly. 'Then I was right to take a break and think things through.' She didn't think their relationship could possibly work in the way Martyn wanted, but maybe she had been pushing herself too hard and hadn't given either of them a proper chance.

There was no time to dwell on things, though, because Ross arrived to see Sam. She pushed the letter back into the pocket of her skirt and showed him into the living room.

'I didn't think you were coming today,' Sam said. 'Not when you didn't arrive this morning. Shouldn't this be your afternoon in the surgery?'

Ross put his briefcase down on the coffee-table. 'My partner and I did a swap. Her husband has been working away, but he's due back this evening and she wanted to finish early. She's planning a celebration meal, I think. It's a tenth anniversary, apparently, so she's preparing the works—candlelight and flowers, chilled wine. Soft music in the background.'

He looked at Heather as he spoke, and for a moment or two she wondered what it would be like to sit across the table from him, with the light dimmed and music playing and a fire glowing in the grate. But then her grandfather coughed chestily and the image vanished, leaving her feeling oddly out of synch. What was she doing, thinking peculiar thoughts like that, anyway?

She looked at Sam in concern. 'Grandad, are you all right?'

He nodded, still wheezing, and Ross went over to him and helped him to a chair.

'You look tired,' he said. 'Sit down and rest.'

'Only to be expected at my age,' Sam said when he had his breath back. 'I'm getting on a bit, you know. You're as bad as Heather. I keep telling her I'm fine, but she worries too much. Like my Jenny, bless her.' His eyes shimmered for a second or two, but it might have been a trick of the light. 'I miss her, you know.'

'I know.' Ross laid a hand on his shoulder. 'Let me take a look at you. How are you getting on with the tablets?'

Heather bit her lip and left them to it, and went to finish clearing up in the kitchen. She had everything tidy by the time Ross was finished, and she was studying the cupboards for supplies that were running short so she could pick some up while she was out.

'He's checking the weather forecast. Wants to know which TV channel gives the best prospect of rain for his plants.'

They laughed together, then he asked, 'How did work go last night? Smoothly? Did you come across any more of my patients?'

Her expression must have given her away because his brow lifted. 'Not so good? Tell me.'

Heather told him about her visit to the Fraser household. 'More of a case of insensible through drink than from the fall.'

He winced. 'It isn't the first time, and it won't be the last. He can be troublesome, a menace sometimes. It's no job for a woman, having to deal with someone like him. Drunks are unpredictable and dangerous—especially ones like Kevin Fraser.'

She eyed him scornfully. 'Patients are patients. We're hardly in the business of being able to pick and choose. You're living in the Dark Ages. If it was left to men like you, I dare say women would still be battling to get a place in medical school.'

'Oh, there are some advantages to the womanly touch. It means you get to deal with the children who've indulged in too much ice cream and candyfloss at the May Fair. If you hadn't stepped into the breach, it might have been down to me. Heaven forbid that I should be the one that they're sick over!'

She sent him a mock glare and made to cuff his ear so that he put up his hands in self-defence.

'OK, I'm going while I'm still in one piece. I'll see you there on Saturday—for my sins, I'm judging the children's fancy dress.'

She grinned. 'That should be fun.'

He rolled his eyes. 'Are you taking Sam with you, or shall I pick him up?'

'He's going with me.' She pulled a wry face. 'He wants to be there at the start to make sure I put his plants on display properly!'

* * *

Heather woke early on the day of the fair. It started off warm, getting warmer, with the clouds disappearing by midday to leave a hot, blue sky in their wake. Glorious! By the time they arrived at the park where the marquees and stands were set up, the sun was beating down relentlessly on everyone and everything in its path.

She gave Sam a long glance, before briefly checking the stall once more and seeing to it that the hamper she'd filled with food and cool drinks was within easy reach. 'Will you be OK here?'

'Of course I will. I've got Fred and Harry here to keep me company. We're not likely to get into any trouble—well, not much, at any rate, not at our age.' He chuckled and she kissed him affectionately on the cheek and left him to it.

'Try to stay under the awning in the shade. I'll be back later on to see how you're doing.' He'd have a fine old time. Most of his friends and neighbours would be along to buy the plants, she guessed, and they would spend the time gossiping together.

She made her way to the first-aid tent, glancing about her to see if Ross was anywhere around. There was no sign of him, and she crossly quelled the odd feeling of disappointment that swelled inside her. She ought to find better things to do than keep thinking about him. The only thing they had in common was his concern for Grandad.

The St John's ambulance crew were in attendance already inside the tent, and Heather exchanged greetings with them, before satisfying herself that everything was in order. The two camp beds were there just in case, but she hoped they wouldn't be needed. More likely, she would have to deal with nothing more than a few grazed knees or a faint or two, judging by this heat. She set out her equipment, checked it over, then settled down to chat and read a book until the first patient came along.

'Damn wasps. They're everywhere.' She was on her own, the others having gone for a break, when a commotion disturbed the quiet towards the middle of the afternoon, and a wailing child, red-faced and not much more than around four years old, was ushered into the tent.

'It's all right, love, the doctor's here—show her your arm.'

The little girl's father urged her forward and presented the child's chubby arm for Heather to see.

Heather crouched down to the girl's level and looked into her watery blue eyes. 'Can I have a look, sweetheart?' There was some swelling and a reddened point where the sting had gone in. 'Oh, yes, there it is.'

She picked up her tweezers and deftly tweaked it out before the child had time to voice an objection. She dropped it into a kidney bowl, then quickly applied a cold compress. 'All over now,' she told the little girl. 'I'll put some antihistamine cream on it,' she told the father. 'That should reduce some of the discomfort. The irritation will probably fade within an hour or so, but see your own doctor if you have any problems.'

The little girl was busy inspecting the sting in the bowl, her eyes wide. 'Is that what stung me?'

Heather smiled. 'Yes. It's out now so your arm should start to feel better.' She brought out a sweet jar from under the table and, after a nod from the father, said, 'Here you are, poppet—have a sweetie, if you like.'

She did like, and went away happily with her relieved parent. Another child came in as she was leaving, and Heather removed a splinter from the boy's tiny finger. She was just cleaning up after he'd gone when she heard someone else arrive, and she looked up to see Ross, standing there.

For a moment her heart made an odd little thump, and her mouth was suddenly dry. He was wearing stone-washed jeans that moulded themselves to his hips and thighs and drew her attention to his long, powerful legs. Her glance trailed upwards and caught the ripple of muscle beneath his cream-coloured T-shirt. Her breath snagged in her throat and she looked away quickly. Toby was with him, panting from the heat but bright-eyed with the fun of being out.

'Are you busy?'

'Not really,' she said, getting her breath back. 'How did the fancy dress go?'

His brows shot up. 'How do you choose? Sit, Toby.' The dog sat, eyed his master, then flopped onto his belly, settling down with his head between his paws but keeping a weather eye on proceedings. 'All those parents, watching you,' Ross went on, 'and willing you to pick their child—the children all desperate to be the one.' He shuddered. 'Never again.'

Heather's grin widened. 'So, how did you cope?'

'I told them all they were so brilliant I didn't know which one to pick. Gave them all a mystery parcel, pink for girls, blue for boys, and picked the robot as winner. Poor little thing deserved it—he was dressed from head to foot in cardboard boxes painted silver and had to be led everywhere by his mum and dad in case he toppled over. I thought he deserved to win, for putting up with that.' He laughed with her and came to prop himself, half sitting, half leaning, on her table. 'No major disasters here, then?'

'Not one. It's been very quiet.' Disturbed by his nearness, she hunted around for equipment to tidy. 'I've had time to go and see that Sam's enjoying himself, and catch up on a bit of reading. Quite relaxing, really, except that most of my patients have been little ones, and it tears me up to see them upset.' The side of her hand knocked against a pair of tweezers and dislodged a box of lint, sending it gliding over the edge of the table.

Ross reached for it at the same moment that she came around to rescue it, and there was a small collision, her arm tangling with his and her breast crushed softly against the wall of his chest.

'Oh!' Fierce flame seemed to shoot through her, melting her insides. Stunned, she was very still for a moment, the blood frantically pulsing through her veins. Dazed, she stared at him in confusion, and the subtle fragrance of his cologne drifted past her nostrils. She tried to move away and swayed slightly.

'I'm sorry...' His hand came out to steady her and settled warmly on the rounded curve of her hip. It felt so good, so natural, that she almost drowned in the sweet sensations that washed over her. She heard his ragged breathing, saw the muscle flicker in his jaw.

'Heather...' he said hoarsely. His gaze meshed with hers, then slid down to linger on the pink fullness of her mouth.

Her lips began to tingle in response. She sank back against the edge of the table and wondered what was happening to her, whether she had completely lost control of her senses. She had always been so practical, so sensible, and now... He bent his head towards her, she stopped breathing and everything around her faded into insignificance.

He was going to kiss her... Weakly, her fingers came up against his chest. 'Ross, I—'

But then there was a disturbance outside and the sound of voices, getting closer. Shakily, she drew back from him. Ross's hand dropped from her hip where it had seemed so perfectly to belong, leaving her feeling oddly deprived, and he turned instead to pick up the fallen box of lint.

'Perhaps I should go,' he said huskily. 'It looks as though you're going to be needed.' His mouth twisted in a kind of grimace. 'I should get back to keep an eye on things.'

He probably meant Grandad. He seemed to be in complete command of himself now, alert and on the move, while she was still floundering, her mind hazy and her heart thumping heavily.

Heather tried desperately to drag her thoughts back to her surroundings, and her glance went to the tent flap where a man was entering, supporting a woman.

'She's had a funny turn, collapsed on me. Can you do something?'

Heather straightened and went over to her patient, breathing deeply and trying hard to slow down her pulse and concentrate on work. 'Lay her down on the bed, and I'll have a look at her.' She was amazed how calm her voice sounded. 'Has she been ill? Does she suffer from anything specific?'

The man raked his black hair with his fingers. 'Nothing at all. Not that I know of. She's always on the go. Doesn't eat properly.'

In control of herself now, Heather made a quick examination. The woman's eyes were closed but she was conscious, her skin moist and cool.

'Have you done a lot of walking today?'

The woman said weakly, 'We were here from the start—didn't want to miss the parade. I went into town this morning.'

'I think you're probably suffering from heat exhaustion. You'll be all right if you rest here a while. I'll get you something to drink. That should do the trick.'

She poured blackcurrant cordial into a glass, and helped the woman to take a few sips until she had recovered enough to manage by herself.

'Shall I sit with her—is it all right if we stay here for a bit?' The man looked anxious and Heather smiled at him.

'Of course it is. Pull up a chair and stay until she feels well enough to go.'

She left them to it, and went and stood in the doorway where there was a faint, cooling breeze, and scanned the crowds for sight of Ross. She was still surprised by the strength of feeling she'd experienced when she had thought he'd been about to kiss her. The aftermath was a peculiar sense of loss, and she found herself wanting to see him again—just a glimpse, that was all.

A dog barked a few yards away, an eager expectant sound, and she turned towards it, to see Toby running in playful circles around a little boy. The child was laughing, his fair hair gleaming where the sun caught it, and Heather smiled, absorbed in the sight of them playing together. He and the dog seemed to know each other.

She watched them for a while until a young woman came towards them, her hair the same bright colour as the boy's, and something about the eyes, too, looking familiar. She was pregnant, about five months, Heather guessed, and her back must have been aching because she pressed her palms into it and stretched wearily.

Then Ross came on the scene, and it was on the tip of Heather's tongue to call his name—except that he put an arm around the woman's shoulder and beckoned to the boy. 'Come on, Ben, we're going home. Mummy needs to put her feet up and rest. Toby, here.' He clicked his fingers and the dog stopped jumping around and ambled to his side. Ben went after him, and the four of them strolled slowly over to the car park.

Heather watched them go, her blood running cold—shock freezing her to the spot. She sank her teeth painfully into her lip and, for some unaccountable reason, felt like weeping.

CHAPTER FIVE

Ross—*married?*

The weekend was behind Heather now, but still the words reverberated inside her head and she was having trouble taking it in. It had come as such a shock.

Heather stared down at the flowerbed she had been working on, without focusing properly on it. Her legs were stiff from kneeling, and she stretched a little to ease the knots of tension in them. Sam came and stood beside her, distracting her as he bent down to pick up the bucket of weeds she had pulled up, and she noticed how slow and laboured his movements were.

'I'll take these up to the compost heap for you,' he said.

'I'll do it, Grandad.' She dragged her mind back to the task in hand. 'Don't you think you've done enough for today?' She was worried about him. His recovery had been slow after his heart attack and she wanted to be able to stay and take care of him, but what would happen when her temporary work here came to an end in a few weeks? Who would look after him then if she went back home? It tore her to shreds emotionally, just thinking about leaving him to manage on his own, no matter how kind his friends and neighbours were. She couldn't do it, could she? But there was the offer of the permanent job back home to consider, and Martyn, and her father, and the flat she'd left empty.

Sam shook his head. 'I want to help.' Heather bit her lip, but thought better of arguing. As Ross had pointed out, it must be frustrating for him, being thwarted by his body's weakness where once he had been so active.

He went off with the bucket, and she leaned back on her heels and wiped the beads of perspiration from her brow with the back of her hand. The sun was fierce again today, just as it had been on the day of fair—the last time she had seen Ross.

She frowned. Why did it bother her so much that he was married? A lump caught in her throat. Not just married, but with a child and another on the way. Somehow that made it all much worse.

Had his wife's pregnancy been the reason he had turned to her? He had been about to kiss her—if they hadn't been interrupted he would have, she felt sure. And she would have responded... A rush of heat swamped her veins just thinking about it. She was still confused about how it had happened. Simply, Ross had touched her and thoughts of anything else had gone completely out of her head.

She had been drawn to him despite her reservations. Over the last week or two she had grown to like Ross and to respect him—for the way he was with Sam, the caring that came across when he talked about his patients, the way he was with her and his gentleness and humour. And now, she sighed heavily, that had all been washed away because now she knew what he really was—a flirt, a womaniser—and she felt empty inside.

Heather attacked the weeds again with new vigour. Things would be a lot easier if she didn't keep running into him every few days. Would it be so difficult to avoid him? Probably...but their meetings could at least be kept on a purely professional level.

'You've worked wonders, girl.' Sam appeared once more at her side and put the empty bucket down. 'The garden's beginning to look good again after all my neglect. It never used to be so difficult to pull it all in.' His expression grew wistful, his glance going to the bench by the pond, and she realised he must be thinking of her grandmother.

She gave him a soft smile. 'Come on, let's go in and get cleaned up. We can leave the rest until tomorrow. There'll be time for us to have a go at the crossword before I have to get ready for work.'

May slid towards June and the heatwave continued, sapping her energy. Or perhaps it was the effort of avoiding Ross that was so draining. On the occasions when they did meet she tried to be distant and professional, and if he was puzzled by the change in her attitude to him at least he didn't push the issue. He was probably too busy to let it bother him. Lately, he had seemed harassed.

'I'll have to rush off,' he said to Sam one afternoon. 'My partner has had to take a few days' leave unexpectedly, and I'm having problems with cover. These last few days have been hectic.'

'That's all right, lad. Me and Heather are doing fine. She's a good lass.'

Ross sent her a thoughtful, considering look and seemed about to say something, but she turned away and busied herself, getting her things together in preparation for work. By the time she'd seen to the evening meal and relaxed in a bath it would be time to go.

It was an eventful night, as it turned out. One of her patients had to be admitted to hospital as an emergency after suffering a stroke, and by the time she'd dealt with all the arrangements and had answered his wife's anxious questions another call had come in from one of the isolated villages.

A woman had gone into labour two months early after a fall, and it was touch and go for a while. The worried husband was trying to look after his wife and pacify their young son, who had woken when he'd heard the commotion. Heather had her work cut out, but she managed to get everything under control and sent for the ambulance. The baby was in a hurry to come into the world, and Heather was wrapping her in a blanket as the ambulance crew arrived.

'The baby's doing fine,' she told the tearful and exhausted young mother. 'She'll need to go straight to Neonatal, but her size and weight mean she should do well in spite of her untimely arrival.'

Mrs Sanderson sagged back against her pillows, white-faced, all her pent-up emotion released in a tide of relief.

'Can I hold her?'

Heather smiled. 'Of course. Just for a minute, though, because I need to check you over.'

The mother would need monitoring as well as the baby. She had haemorrhaged and Heather had been worried for a while, but she had managed to stem the bleeding and get the patient's condition stabilised. The rest was up to the hospital.

She sighed wearily and stretched her aching limbs. She wouldn't be sorry to see the end of this shift.

About half an hour before it was due to finish, though, there was another call, this time to one of the cottages near her grandfather's home.

'I'm really glad you could come out, Doctor.' The woman who showed Heather into the house looked pale and tired, and Heather guessed she must have been up for much of the night. 'I'm sorry it's so early but my husband looks ill—feverish. We thought it was flu or something but he's been cough, cough, cough, all night.'

The man was in bed, looking haggard and drained.

'Are you bringing something up?' Heather asked, and when he nodded she went on, 'What colour was it?'

'Brownish, sort of.'

Heather examined him. His temperature was certainly raised, and there was a lot of congestion on his lungs.

'Hmm.' She put her stethoscope away. 'It sounds as though you have a chest infection, John, but I'd like you to have an X-ray just to make sure. I'll give you some antibiotics in the meantime, and you can take paracetamol to bring down your temperature. Try to drink plenty of cool fluids as well.'

She wrote out a form for the X-ray department and handed it to him. 'Take this with you, and go and see your doctor in a week's time for the results.'

John Laughton nodded, and Heather went downstairs and spoke to his wife again, before leaving for home. Her limbs were protesting with weariness, and the chance to grab a few hours' sleep was uppermost in her mind.

It was early in the afternoon before Heather felt sufficiently on form again, and she decided that, since Sam was spending the day with a friend, she might as well go down to the shops and see if she could find some paint that would look good on the walls of the spare bedroom. Grandad had said it needed doing.

On the way to town she passed Ross's surgery, and she felt a curious urge to stop and give it a second glance. It was a big house with a deep, sloping roof, wide windows, fronted by a paved area set aside for parking, and enclosed by low stone walls. The whole of it was beautifully landscaped with trees and flowering shrubs.

Since she was here she may as well hand over her notes on the night's visits to the receptionist. At this time of day Ross would most probably be taking surgery, or out on call, so there wasn't much likelihood that she would run into him.

She was wrong about that, as it turned out. Before Heather could stop her, Julie Brant in Reception had pressed the button on the intercom and was saying briefly, 'Dr Kennedy, Dr Brooks is here. Did you want a word?'

His reply was muffled to Heather's ears, but the woman gave a quick smile and said, 'He'll be along in a second or two, Dr Brooks. It's nice to meet you at last. We think the world of your grandfather, you know. He's lived round here for a good many years, hasn't he?'

'As far back as I can remember,' Heather acknowledged. 'Look, I didn't mean to stay. I just wanted to leave some notes for Dr Kennedy.'

She felt trapped. The last thing she wanted was to see Ross or, worse, run into his wife. She was too late, though, to change things. Even as she opened her roomy leather bag to take out her papers Ross appeared in a doorway, looking pleased to see her.

'Come through to the back, Heather. I was just finishing a late lunch—it's been non-stop here for the last hour or so. I've been out on call all morning, and then there was another stack of post to go through. Hospital test results and reports from various consultants.' His glance moved over her. 'Are you hungry? There's salad—and fruit.'

'No, thanks. I'm not hungry, I've already eaten. I only came to drop off some notes—I was on my way to town,' she began, trying to excuse herself and make her escape. But his arm came warmly around her, his palm flat on the small of her back, and before she could finish saying her piece she was being ushered into the living rooms at the rear of the surgery. The mere fact that his arm was around her was enough to send everything out of her head.

'You can show them to me in comfort,' he said. 'We haven't had the chance to talk for a while—not properly, anyway,' he said, giving her a disarming grin. His dog came bounding forward to greet her, his tail swishing joyfully. 'Down, Toby,' Ross ordered good-naturedly. 'Have some decorum.'

There was no sign of his wife or Ben, but perhaps the boy was at nursery school.

'I shouldn't stay—you must be busy,' Heather said quickly, but he shook his head and showed her into the living room.

'I've a good half an hour before my next patient arrives. Make yourself at home.'

Heather gave in and stroked the dog's silky head, then looked around the spacious room. It was warm and inviting, comfortably furnished with big easy chairs and a wide, soft-cushioned settee. Sunlight poured in through glazed doors that opened out onto a small terrace, overlooking the garden.

'Oh, Ross, this is lovely,' she said, taking it all in— the shades of colour that reflected the sun, the paintings on the walls, the flowers arranged in delightful profusion on the window sill and on a small polished cabinet.

He was pleased with her reaction to his home. 'Sit down, here on the sofa...' He patted a cushion and she did as she was told, still glancing around. 'I'll go and get an extra cup, and then you can show me those notes. I brought the teatray in here while I went over some papers.'

He was back in a flash, and when he sat down beside her she started to tell him about John Laughton and the X-ray. Anything to take her mind off his nearness.

'I'll see it's followed up,' he said. 'There's still no news on Richard Stanway—the young man with the spinal problem—but his hospital appointment has been arranged.' He swallowed his drink then asked, 'How's Sam? Any improvement?'

She shook her head, her mouth and eyes giving away her sadness. 'I wish there was something more we could do, but it was a bad attack and his strength seems to be failing. I hate to see him like that. I just wish—' She broke off and Ross sent her a considering glance.

'What? That you could stay on here? He does need someone close.'

'I know…but my job here finishes soon and I haven't seen anything else advertised locally. I thought of asking him to come home with me, but I know he would never leave the cottage.'

Ross put his cup down and leaned towards her. 'There is something you could do…' She looked at him questioningly and he went on, 'You remember I told you that my partner's husband had been away recently?'

Heather nodded, and he said, 'Well, it appears his firm wants him to relocate to Scotland. It's an opportunity that's too good to miss, apparently, but of course it leaves Tessa with a bit of a dilemma. She wants to join him as soon as possible but it would leave me in a difficult position. It isn't always easy to find someone suitable to fill the gap at short notice.'

His gaze held hers steadily. 'If you were to consider taking on the job, though, I'm pretty sure we'd make a good team. I know how you work, and I know the people round here think highly of you.' He smiled at her. 'Word gets around. Not only from patients you've visited in the area, but people who were at the May Fair have been singing your praises ever since. So…' he reached out and took her hand in his, sending a thrill of warmth racing along her arm '…what do you think? Will you consider taking the job on?'

Heather's mind was in a whirl. It looked as though he was offering her a brilliant solution, but how could she think straight when he was holding her and looking at her like that, his eyes gleaming—willing her to say yes?

His thigh brushed hers inadvertently and sent a shock wave of heat coursing through her. She eased away from him and tried to pull her thoughts together. What was

his real motive? Was it a carefully thought-out propo-
sition, or did he have other things in mind? She didn't
think she could bear it if it was just a ploy to get close.
She didn't want to think badly of him, but her confidence
in him was badly dented.

'I don't know,' she said hesitantly. She needed to
think. How could she work with him every day when
she was so conscious of him all the time, knowing that
he was a married man? But what choice was there, at
the end of the day? There was her grandfather to consider, and that ought to take precedence over everything.

'What's the problem?' His expression was serious.

'We don't know if we can work together—you have
your ideas about things and I have mine. We might
clash. It might not work out.'

His mouth twitched. 'You're putting difficulties in the
way before we've even started—is it such a weighty
prospect to consider? You're exactly right for the job. I
need a woman doctor to balance things. From what Sam
told me, you've specialised in all the relevant areas—
gynaecology, obstetrics, paediatrics. Your being here is
a godsend.'

'Sam told you that?'

He spread his hands. 'He's always talking about you.
He's proud of you. I think he'd love you to stay.'

Her insides twisted. It was what she wanted, too, but
there was more to consider than that. She'd have a job
convincing her father that she was doing the right thing.
A city practice, with Martyn on hand, was what he en-
visaged. But when it came down to the nitty-gritty it
was her life, her decision.

'This is all so unexpected.' Her eyes were troubled.
'There's my flat back home—I'd never intended coming
here for any length of time.'

'Couldn't you rent it out through a reliable agency?'
He paused, seeing her hesitate. 'If you're concerned, we

could make it a temporary arrangement—see how things go initially. Three months, perhaps?'

Three months—time for her to be with Sam, and time for her to think over the situation and make up her mind. It seemed a fair plan.

Slowly she nodded. 'OK. You've talked me into it.'

'Good girl.' His hands curved about her arms, and he gave her a hug, dropping a firm kiss on her startled mouth. Her lips burned from the brief contact, and when he released her she had to resist the urge to press her fingers to her tingling flesh. 'You won't regret it, I promise.' He was looking down at her, his mouth tilted in an attractive smile that made her insides flutter wildly. She was beginning to regret her decision already.

'We'll sort out the details later,' he said. 'Want to celebrate with a glass of something? There's a bottle of plonk in the fridge, I think.'

She shook her head. 'I shouldn't—I'm driving.' Then a bell rang somewhere in the house, and Ross groaned.

'I'd almost forgotten afternoon surgery. Sure I can't tempt you?'

She wasn't at all sure. Temptation was definitely the word where he was concerned, but it was something she was determined to fight.

'Go and see to your patients,' she murmured, standing up. 'I have to go into town, anyway.'

He went with her to see her out to the car. 'I'll bring a bottle with me next time I come over to Sam's place, and we'll cement the deal.'

He arrived at the weekend, true to his word, with a bottle of wine and a bunch of peach roses in delicate bud that immediately stole her heart.

'They're beautiful—you shouldn't have.' She was with Sam in the garden, where she was attempting to repair the broken fence post with new wood, inexpertly hammering nails in position. She was acutely conscious of her casual dress—denims and a cotton shirt, clothing suitable for the job in hand. That shouldn't matter, though—this was purely business. All the same, she sniffed at the flowers, drinking in their subtle, sweet scent. 'I'll put these in some water.' She made for the kitchen, and Ross turned to chat to Sam.

When she came back, holding her tray loaded with sandwiches, he was finishing the job of fixing the new posts in place, and she said quickly, 'There's no need for you to do that—I was managing just fine.' She put down the tray and set the wine glasses out on the garden table.

'So you were.' He grinned, and carried on hammering. He had rolled up his shirtsleeves, and she watched him work, his strong hands and muscled arms making it seem an effortless task and thoroughly male territory. She blinked away the sensual, sexy imagery.

'I'm perfectly capable of putting a few bits of wood in position,' she protested.

'No one's arguing the point.' He studied her battle stance, a hint of amusement pulling at his mouth. 'There's no sense in putting calluses on those soft hands, though. Mine are already tough.'

'It doesn't occur to you that sometimes a woman might prefer a challenge? Hadn't you thought of that?'

His brows lifted. 'Are you a feminist?'

Her grandfather chuckled. 'Don't get her started on that one, Ross. All her life she's battled with her father on that issue. Robert Brooks has very decided ideas on a woman's place—and it never fails to cause sparks when he and Heather get together.'

'Hardly surprising, is it, when you think about the way my mother had her ambitions squashed?' Heather retorted. 'If she'd done what she'd wanted she'd have gone in for a nursing career, instead of being made to play the part of a submissive wife, always at my father's beck and call.'

'Aren't you being a bit hard on him?' Ross put the last post in place and ran his glance over her.

Heather shrugged. 'It's all a matter of perspective. My mother often felt stifled—that's why she came here to stay with my nan and grandad. Those were the times she felt really happy. We were all happy, away from his dominating influence.'

Sam handed Ross a nail and said wheezily, 'We did have some good times, but it wasn't just that Jane wanted time to herself. She wanted Heather and her brother to spend time in the country, breathing fresh air and seeing a different life to the town.'

'Sounds to me as though Heather, at least, acquired a love of the country,' Ross said, 'since she's set on staying for a while.' He stood back to look at his handiwork, then dusted his hands on his trousers. 'Time to open the wine, I think, and drink to the future.'

He popped the cork on the wine and poured a glass for each of them. They drank a toast and Heather saw that Sam was beaming with pleasure, and that made it all worthwhile. It was good to see him happy. Her own misgivings could be put on hold. She'd face up to each situation as it arose.

Her work at the surgery started a couple of weeks after that. She put in an appearance early on her first day, wanting to familiarise herself with everything before surgery began.

Ross was out on call, but Julie in Reception knew the ropes well enough to guide her through, and there was back-up in the form of a nurse practitioner, Shannon, and the district nurse, a sturdy, wholesome woman of around forty who competently dealt with the people who were housebound.

Heather settled herself at the desk in the room Tessa had vacated and rang for her first patient.

'Come in, Mrs Lansdowne, and have a seat. What can I do for you?'

Mrs Lansdowne showed her the rash on her fingers, the whole area red and irritable-looking with a crusted, scaly appearance.

'It's itching me to death,' the woman said. 'Nothing I put on it seems to make it go away. I've tried hand cream, antiseptic cream, but it just goes on spreading.'

'It could be caused by any number of things you come into contact with,' Heather murmured, inspecting the rash. 'Do you use rubber gloves when you wash up?'

Mrs Lansdowne shook her head. 'Should I, do you think?'

'I think it would be help. Try to keep your hands dry—see that they don't get moist or sweaty. I can give you a mild steroid cream which should help to clear it up, but continue to use the gloves afterwards to prevent it coming back again. You might find that some hand creams start it off—the perfumes in them can cause trouble in susceptible people.'

Her next patient came in, looking stiff and tense, and Heather was surprised to realise that she had met her before.

'Hello, Mrs Fraser. How can I help?'

'I haven't been sleeping properly lately. I keep having nightmares all the time and I wake up feeling exhausted.' She was clenching her fingers as she spoke, not looking properly at Heather, and there was a restlessness about her as though she was going to jump up at any time— as though sitting still was a problem.

'And how are you coping in the daytime?' Heather asked.

Mrs Fraser shook her head. 'I'm not. Not at all, really. It's frightening. I've been having attacks—panicky feelings, I suppose—and my head feels peculiar, I get dizzy and my chest feels tight. I think I'm going to pass out. It hurts, and it scares me. I can't think, I can't eat, I can't stay in the house.'

Heather could imagine what the basis of her problem was, but she asked all the same, 'Do you know what brings on these episodes?'

The woman shrugged, pushing her hand distractedly through her hair. 'It's everything just lately. The bills keep mounting up. Kev's been threatened with the sack because he's had so much time off with the drinking. Then Natalie left home and I don't blame her. Why would she stay, with things as they are? It's just—I used to at least be able to talk to her. Now, I just feel so alone. It never seems to end.'

Heather reached for her prescription pad. 'I can give you something to help you over for the next month. Take one tablet twice a day. It should help to stop the worst effects of the panic attacks. Try to eat sensibly in the meantime, small meals, if that's all you can manage, but at regular intervals—and avoid things like tea, coffee or cola just before bedtime. Have a milky drink instead.'

She smiled sympathetically at the woman. 'I know it's hard, but try not to think over your problems when you get to bed. Sometimes it helps to change your routine a little, do something different. Couldn't you go and see Natalie, or phone her? I expect she'd be glad of your support. She's probably missing you, too.'

Mrs Fraser nodded. 'I hadn't thought of it that way. I didn't want to intrude, but I do know where she's living. I could phone her and arrange to go over there.'

Heather went over to the shelves on the opposite wall and took some leaflets down from a file. 'These might help to give you some ideas on how to deal with stress. Come and see me again in a fortnight.'

Mrs Fraser took the leaflets and the prescription and went to the door. 'Thanks.'

Things went on smoothly for the rest of the morning. Heather had a cup of coffee after half an hour or so, then worked on until it was almost lunchtime and her last patient, a baby, about eighteen months old, came into the room with his mother.

'He keeps being sick,' Mrs Barrett said anxiously. 'He hasn't kept any of his food down at all today.'

'Has he had any diarrhoea?'

The mother nodded, and Heather gently examined the fretful child, noting the slightly shrunken fontanelle.

'Poor little cherub, you must be feeling miserable.' To Mrs Barrett she said, 'Don't give him any food for the next twenty-four hours, and keep him off milk. He's dehydrated so he does need to drink plenty of fluids. I'll prescribe some sachets of rehydrating medicine that you can add to cooled, boiled water.'

She picked up her notes and saw Mrs Barrett to the door, opening it just as Ross came back from his calls.

Distracted, the baby stopped grizzling and made a grab for Heather's curls with a chubby fist, making both women laugh. Still smiling, Heather gently released her hair and walked to the empty waiting room alongside Ross.

'I expect it was the sun falling on your hair that caught his attention,' Ross said with a grin. 'It's very eye-catching, gloriously gold. I've always thought your hair was a splendid colour—a sort of dark honey with trapped sunlight. Seems I'm not alone in thinking that.'

Heather put her notes down on the counter and busied herself, checking the diary. Perhaps if she filled her mind with work she wouldn't have to try so hard to keep him out of it.

'How did it go this morning?' he asked. 'Any problems?'

'None at all,' she told him briskly. 'Everything seemed to go very well. A few people were curious about the new doctor, I thought, but they were all very nice.' She glanced around the waiting room, clean and bright with a soft blue flecked carpet and matching grey-blue upholstered chairs and low tables with neatly stacked magazines.

'What do you think?' Ross asked, watching her. 'Will it do?'

She nodded. 'It's comfortable-looking—just about right—and the pictures are a nice touch, but I'd like to see some more toys for the children. A corner set aside specially, perhaps, with things that are unbreakable and easy to clean, preferably.'

'We could arrange that easily enough. I'll get some catalogues for you to browse through, and you can choose what you want.'

'What are you buying?' The outside door clattered open, and the little boy, Ben, came into the room, followed by his mother. Heather's stomach twisted, but she tried to put on a welcoming smile.

'Toys for the waiting room,' Ross said, smiling down at the boy. 'What should we get, do you think?'

Ben thought about it. 'Lego,' he said, 'and cars and trains and wheely things—some building bricks and a slide and some tractors and some big lorries with tippers on the back.'

He paused to take a breath, and his mother said with a laugh, 'Well, that takes care of whatever the boys might want.' She turned to Heather and added, 'You must be our new doctor. I'm glad to meet you, Heather. I'm Louise. You'll have to excuse me for a minute but I simply must go and put this shopping down in the kitchen. I'm bushed.' She stretched her aching back and

Ross took the bags from her. 'Will you stay for lunch?' Louise asked.

Heather shook her head, not trusting herself to impose on this scene of happy domesticity without giving away some of her emotional turmoil.

'I can't, I'm afraid, but thanks very much for the offer. I promised I'd go home and tell Grandad all about my first morning here and share lunch with him.' She backed towards the door as she said it, giving a small wave to Ben on the way. 'Nice to have met you all. I'll catch you later, perhaps.'

Ross frowned, as though he would have asked her to stay but had thought better of it, and she made her escape without too much hassle. She went outside and sat in the car quietly for a moment to calm herself down before she dared drive.

These next few months were going to be even harder to get through than she had imagined. Whenever she was near him she felt drawn to him in some indefinable way, but she couldn't allow her feelings to get the better of her. There were so many reasons why she should avoid him, and most important of all was the fact that he was a married man. She had to remember that.

He was just a colleague, nothing more, and if she told herself that often enough she might eventually come to believe it.

CHAPTER SIX

THE ambulance dropped Sam at home after his physio session and Heather helped him out into the garden. She had set the lunch out on the patio table so that they could enjoy the sunshine.

'You look cheerful,' she said, watching the twinkle in his eyes as he slowly reached forward and helped himself to chicken and rice.

'It's being with the other crocks for the last couple of hours,' he told her with a chuckle. 'Makes me feel less of an invalid and more like part of the club.' He reached for the salad bowl. 'How did your morning go? Do you think you'll like working there?'

There was an eager, hopeful note in his voice, and she smiled and answered easily, 'I'm sure I shall.' She told him all about her first impressions of the place, keeping it light, and he listened carefully while he tucked into his meal.

'Do you think you and Ross will get along?' he said, frowning a little. 'He likes his own way, but he always seems to have his heart in the right place.'

She glanced at him, pushing away her plate and taking an apple from a dish. 'We'll get along just fine,' she said with a conviction she didn't entirely feel. How difficult could it be? All she had to do was keep everything on a purely professional footing between them, and having Louise and Ben on the scene should make that a whole lot easier.

She made a faint grimace. Louise was a warm, friendly person who deserved better than to have her husband flirting on the side, and from what she'd seen of Ben he was a lovely child, open and guileless, the sort of boy she'd have wanted for her own.

A strong wave of emotion surged through her and she was very still, the apple poised a fraction of an inch away from her lips. The idea that she might one day have children was something that she'd pushed to one side, but now she felt an aching sense of loss. Was she right to go on being so set against marriage? She had never really been convinced that any relationship stood a fair chance of success in the long term—look at the Frasers and how their marriage had been turned into a battle zone. What chance did their daughter have of making a go of things, unmarried and pregnant and forced to leave home?

She bit into the apple, and Sam said gruffly, 'I expect that fella of yours will want to know why you're not going home to him. Shouldn't be surprised if he comes down here to fetch you back.'

Was that worrying him—the thought that she might be persuaded to change her mind? Heather got to her feet and gave him a hug. 'Can't be done,' she told him, starting to clear the table. 'I've signed a contract so I'm here to stay—for the next few months at least. I'm going to stay and take care of you. I've written home and told them all what the situation is.'

Martyn hadn't liked it at all. His last letter had been full of expressions of disbelief and recriminations that she wasn't about to pack up and rush to his side, but she refused to let the guilt get to her. She had tried to be honest with him about how she felt. If he really cared for her, wouldn't he come to understand what was important to her? She had to be true to her conscience, didn't she?

She sighed, and took the crockery into the kitchen. There was no time to think about it now. She ought to be getting back to work to start her afternoon clinic, and she could only hope that she wouldn't run into Ross or his wife.

'What are you planning on doing this afternoon?' She asked Sam when she had finished clearing away and they were back in the house.

'Frank's coming over in about half an, hour,' he said. 'He thinks he's going to beat me at Scrabble.'

Heather shared a grin with him, then kissed him affectionately and set off for the surgery once more to prepare for her child health clinic.

The child health checks were a part of the job she liked best. Seeing the young mothers with their offspring always lifted her spirits, and at least she didn't have to do the immunisations. They might well be the best medicine, but the tots didn't always seem to appreciate that at the time!

She worked steadily through her list, giving out teddy-bear stickers along the way, and an hour or so later saw the last of her small charges out of the door.

'Bring Chloe into the surgery next week, Mrs Harrison, and I'll listen to her chest again to see if it's clear.'

The mother and child went off, and Heather turned towards Reception, walking headlong into Ross as he emerged from his room. The soft impact made her stumble backwards, and his hands came out to grasp her warmly, driving everything from her mind. Her fingers clutched at his jacket and missed, sliding down to rest flatly on his chest. He was very close, and she caught the merest drift of a subtle cologne mingled with something more, his own essential maleness. Through his shirt she felt the steady beat of his heart and the warmth that came from his skin.

'I didn't see you—I wasn't expecting—' Winded a little, her words came out raggedly.

'I'm sorry—are you all right? It was my fault, I was

too busy thinking about something to look where I was going.' His palm brushed her spine and settled distractingly on the soft swell of her hip.

She tried to ignore the tide of heat that swept through her from head to toe at his touch. 'I'm fine.' She swallowed, and made an attempt to recover her poise. 'What were you thinking about? Is it anything I can help you with?'

'Possibly. Have you finished your clinic? We could take a walk, get a breath of air, if you like.'

At least if they were walking it would be less intimate than being cooped up with him here. 'That sounds like a good idea. I could do with stretching my legs.'

He nodded, pleased, then called to Toby, who came out from the kitchen and trotted up to them, his tail wagging.

She had expected Ross to release her as they went along the hall, but his hand stayed distractingly in place until they reached the front door and he held it open for her.

'Which way?' she asked when they were out in the open and she could breath easily again.

'Along the lane, towards the farm and then back via the river?' he suggested, and she nodded, falling into step beside him. He threw a stick for Toby, who raced off after it.

'I wish I had his energy,' she laughed. 'At the end of the day I'm usually too whacked to dash anywhere.'

He grinned. 'Goes with the territory, I suppose. It'll take you a while to get used to working days again.'

'That's true enough. My body clock is all to pot.'

'It doesn't show. But, then, you always look good whatever the time of day.' His glance moved over her, and she felt a blush start up all over again. The corners of his mouth tilted. 'I'm only surprised some man hasn't come along before now and snatched you up out of circulation and kept you busy, looking after a brood of children.'

She gave him a long look. 'What makes you think it hasn't been tried?'

He raised a brow at that. 'And…?'

Her shoulders lifted. 'What would happen to my career? All those years of training… It's different for men, I suppose, since they don't have the babies. Their professional life just gathers momentum and they still manage to go home and enjoy having a family.'

'Some women juggle both.'

Toby came back with the stick and dropped it at Ross's feet, panting for more.

'And some might find that too difficult. It could come down to a plain either-or—career or marriage.'

'Not necessarily.' He bent to pick up the stick and throw it into the distance. 'If the right man was to come along…'

The right man… She shook away the disturbing thought. Perhaps there would never be a right man for her. After all, Martyn was a decent man—he had a lot of fine qualities. He was hard-working, intelligent, interesting to be with…but she still couldn't overcome her reluctance to commit herself to him. She frowned. What was she doing, anyway, letting Ross confuse the issue? She didn't want to be married and lose her independence.

'How does Louise feel about staying home and having the children?' she asked bluntly.

He didn't seem at all fazed by her question. 'I think she's contented enough. She's very good with Ben—always has time to do things with him. This pregnancy is more troublesome than the last, though, and she's often tired so I expect she'd be happier if John was home more to share the burden.'

'John?' Heather blinked, her step faltering on a

crooked paving slab, and his hand shot out to support
her arm.

'Her husband. He's a rep for a pharmaceutical company, which means he has to travel a fair bit and sometimes he's away overnight.'

She let out a long, slow breath, and he studied her,
his dark brows coming together. 'Is something wrong?'

She shook her head and laughed. 'No, nothing at all.'
Then she admitted sheepishly, 'I thought she was your
wife—that Ben was your child. Whenever I saw you you
were together, like a family.'

He laughed with her, a warm sound that slid over her
like honey and brown sugar, smoothing the rough edges
of her nerves. 'Good Lord, no. She's my sister. I'm not
married. It might be better if I was, from my patients'
point of view, respectability, standing in the community
and all that, but it hasn't happened.

'Even if I had time to fraternise, I've never met anyone I wanted to settle down with. I'm too committed to
the job and, anyway, what woman wants to put up with
all the hours a doctor works and suffer all the interrup-
tions and emergencies that crop up? Most women want
work and home to be separate. There isn't much chance
of that here.'

'Not all women think that way.' Despite her relief in
finding that he wasn't married, and that he wasn't in any
way two-timing or untrustworthy, she had a struggle to
stem the inexplicable wave of emotion that swept over
her when she thought about the women in his life. It was
curiosity, she told herself, that was all—a perfectly natural curiosity. He was young, good-looking and su-
premely male. He must have had plenty of opportunity
to get involved.

His shoulders lifted. 'No, they don't. Some just like
the idea of being married to a doctor for the status they
imagine it will bring.'

'And you don't see yourself in that light—a doctor as some kind of power figure?' She'd heard it said before and it had always disturbed her that people could feel that way.

'Heavens, no!' He laughed again, then sobered. 'The reality is far too painful. Having to console sick people, getting sicker while they're on waiting lists that get longer and longer because funding doesn't stretch far enough…standing helplessly by as someone with a terminal illness breathes their last. You know the truth of it.' His expression was sombre and his eyes bleak for a moment or two until he pulled himself up, and tacked on in a brighter vein, 'Still, there's always the other side—the successes. The charity do on Saturday afternoon, for instance.'

She frowned. 'Should I know about it?'

'Don't you? It's a barbecue at the Horse and Groom in aid of the cardiac care unit. The landlord is one of Sam's cronies—another heart victim, but his recovery has been a lot better than Sam's. It'll be fun—as long as someone else is doing the cooking I'm more than happy to go along. You'll come, won't you? I could pick you and Sam up.'

She nodded. 'It sounds as though it will be fun. It'll be good to see him with his friends. I only hope he's feeling up to it. He tries to hide it from me, but he tends to look really frail these days.'

Ross grimaced. 'There's very little we can do, given the damage to his heart. He isn't strong enough for any kind of operation. I wish things could have been different. That's one of the things I was mulling over when we bumped into each other. In Sam's case there's not much more we can do, except make him comfortable and hope that he gets stronger, but maybe we can do more for our other patients than at present.

'We're pretty hard-pressed at the surgery and we're

running as many clinics as we can manage, but I wondered if there was some way we could get the idea of preventative medicine across to our patients more strongly than we have done up to now. The leaflets are always out for people to look at, but how do we get them to take note?'

Heather thought it over, absently stroking Toby's silky ears. Perhaps it was just as well that the conversation had moved on from personal issues. Ross was serious now, his mind on work, and she forced herself to concentrate.

'People look at the information when they're already suffering, I suppose—when it's too late.' She frowned, then said, 'Maybe we could concentrate on one topic for a certain length of time. We could set up an area of the waiting room with a particular display each month—say, healthy eating to begin with, followed by something like an anti-smoking campaign. We'd need to plan specifics.'

'Good idea.' He shot her a wide smile. 'We'll talk it through at the next staff meeting, bring everyone in on it.'

She nodded, her mind abstracted. That was it, wasn't it? She was staff, part of the workforce, and they were colleagues, professionals. She ought to remember that, hadn't she? It shouldn't be too difficult. Wasn't that exactly how she wanted it to be?

The next few days were busy, albeit fairly routine, and the only blot on the horizon was a phone call about the baby with the tummy bug, who seemed not to be making much progress.

'He won't drink the medicine,' his mother said. 'I've made up several of the sachets, but he's refused every one. I've done what you said and kept him off food for the first twenty-four hours except for a biscuit or two, but he's no better and I think he's losing weight.'

'Oh, poor little thing,' Heather said. 'I don't think it's likely to be anything more than a stubborn case of enteritis, but we'd better send off a sample from his nappy to the lab for tests. Come into the surgery and pick up a sterile container from Reception. In the meantime, try giving him plenty of fluids as before—blackcurrant juice or apple juice will be fine but not ice-cold, and avoid milk. If he's losing weight he really needs to eat something so let him have foods like rice, potato, chicken, plenty of fruit and vegetables. Avoid anything with wheat, just to be on the safe side, and we'll follow up the results of the tests in two or three days.'

Saturday came before she had time to draw breath. She finished morning surgery and went home to find Grandad talking to her brother in the kitchen, the pair of them looking happy to be together. Her mouth widened in a smile.

'James! I'd no idea you were coming over,' she said, giving him a hug. 'How long are you here for?'

'Just a flying visit, I'm afraid. I was just telling Grandad I wish I could stay longer, but I'll have to go back tonight or first thing in the morning at the latest. Laura's taken the children off to her mother's for the day, which left me free to come down here, but I have to finish off some reports for work before Monday.'

'Dad's still driving you hard, then?'

James nodded, and they shared a rueful glance. 'It gets Laura down sometimes. She doesn't see why I can't spend more time at home, and she gets resentful.' He paused for a moment or two and Heather sensed he was troubled, that there was a lot more he wanted to say, but he shook himself and went on, 'I don't see that I have any option, not with a mortgage round my neck and the children growing so fast and needing so much. I can't afford to get on the wrong side of Dad…but you know how it is.'

Heather nodded. 'The company has always been his priority. Family tradition and all that.' There was more on James's mind, she guessed, but she thought better of asking him about it now. Later perhaps.

'At least you're here now,' Sam said. 'And you'll enjoy the barbecue—it'll give you a chance to relax. We'll fix up a bed for you in the spare room, and send you off with a good breakfast inside you tomorrow. No reason for you to dash off tonight.'

James grinned. 'Sounds good to me.'

They talked for an hour or so longer, and then Heather went upstairs to change into something more casual. It was another hot day, with very little breeze. It was too hot for jeans so she put on a softly draped skirt and cotton top and fixed her hair back with combs for coolness.

Ross came for them at two, and he and James took to each other straight away, which gave her a warm feeling even though things had turned out just as she'd expected. Most people took to Ross.

'It seems to have done Sam good, seeing your brother,' Ross remarked later, when they had piled up their plates with food and were sitting in a quiet spot by the river that meandered around the back of the pub.

They were alone for a while as Sam had taken James to look around. Behind them there was the sound of children's laughter as they jumped on a huge bouncy castle or played on the swings. Heather had slipped off her shoes and was enjoying the feel of the grass beneath her toes and sniffing the scent of roses that mingled with the faint tang of the barbecue.

'I think James would like to stay on. It might be what he needs, too—a change, a bit of a break, but it doesn't look as though he's going to get one.' She bit into a kebab, tasting the juice of a tender mushroom.

'At least he doesn't look quite as tense as he did earlier.'

Heather glanced at him. 'You noticed it too?'

'There was something about his neck and shoulders, a kind of stiffness, as though he's used to carrying a burden around with him. Overworked, perhaps?'

'Possibly. He tries so hard to keep on the right side of my father. Dad put so much store in his joining the family firm and keeping the family name going through the generations. I expect he has visions of the grandchildren joining the company too eventually.'

'Don't you think that's a good idea? Is your father asking too much, wanting his family to share in something he created? His motives sound reasonable enough—family wealth, loyalty, tradition.'

'Put like that, it does sound reasonable, but you don't know my father—he has an overwhelming personality. He thinks he's right all the time, that his view is the only one.'

'So you never thought about joining the firm—or didn't he want you to? Is it just the male line that he's interested in?'

'Oh, he wanted me to be part of it.' She grimaced. 'I could see what would happen, though. All he really wanted was to be in control, and eventually he would have taken away any initiative I might have had. I didn't think I could cope with that. I've always been too independent.' Her expression was rueful. 'He's never really forgiven me for that decision.'

'Perhaps you misjudged him. He might have valued your intelligence, and had your interests at heart.'

She shook her head. 'I don't think so. He never really liked me very much, you know,' she added soberly. 'There was never any love.'

She caught his shocked expression and shrugged, lifting her hands in a gesture of wry acceptance as she answered his unspoken question. 'I don't know why. I never really understood but I'm sure my instinct is right. I used to try so hard to please him but it was impossible. He never took my side in anything or showed me that he was proud of me. Everything I did was wrong.

When James and I had the accident at the demolition site I was very scared. I'd almost suffocated under the dust and rubble, I was cut and bleeding and I just managed to crawl into the pipe to escape, only to be terrified out of my wits by that dog. James was beside himself with worry. He and his friends drove the dog away with sticks and planks and whatever they could lay their hands on, but I know he blamed himself for what happened. He was the oldest and he thought Dad would flay him alive because he had taken me along with them.

'I told him I'd say it was my idea but, in fact, Dad shouted me down. He ranted and raved, and he blamed me anyway. I was wilful, he said, stubborn and obstinate, always getting into scrapes, and I deserved every bit of what had happened to me, and it was lucky for me that James hadn't been hurt, too.'

Ross's mouth compressed, and a muscle flickered along the line of his jaw. 'He never had any problem with James, then? Did it bother you that your brother had preferential treatment?'

'Not really. James and I have always got on well together, stood by each other in difficult times. I just wish that I could help James now. He isn't saying too much about life back home, he's keeping it close to his chest, but I have the feeling that things aren't going too well between him and Laura. I'd have expected her to come along with him.'

'Maybe she will next time.'

'Maybe.' Heather sat quietly for a moment, deep in

thought, then nibbled at the remains of her kebab. 'Mmm, this is good.' She finished it off, pushed her plate away and began to lick her fingers clean one by one.

Ross watched her, amusement and a hint of something else glinting in his eyes. 'You know, you have the knack of making a simple act look incredibly sensual.'

'Do I? Heavens...' She flushed, heat running along her cheek-bones, then she chuckled ruefully. 'You did bring me here to have fun, didn't you?'

'Definitely.' He leaned towards her. 'Is it having the desired effect?'

'Mmm.' She stretched lazily, arching her spine sinuously like a cat, her mouth curving. 'I think it is.'

'You've worked hard, trying to look after Sam in the day and keep on with the night work, then having to adjust to this new schedule. It was high time you had a break. It's good to watch you relax, to see you smile— like the sun coming out from behind a cloud. In fact,' he added with a gleam, 'it makes you the most gorgeous woman for miles around.'

She studied him from under gold tipped lashes. 'For miles around... I'm not quite sure how to take that. You did say you hadn't been around much lately, didn't you?'

He laughed, a gentle, rumbling sound from deep in his chest. 'Are you trying to tell me I'm not sincere?' His expression changed, became coaxingly intimate. 'Believe me, I am. You won't succeed in putting me off, no matter how you try.' His arm slid around her waist, his breath lightly fanning her cheek. 'I can be very persistent.'

It was fun, just light-hearted banter, but his warmth and nearness were having an unsettling effect on her, undermining her resolve to steer clear of involvement.

'That might not be a good idea,' she mumbled. He was just flirting with her, he didn't mean any of it, and she mustn't let go of all her sensible plans. None of this was real. In a few short months she would be moving on, back to city life and a different pace… Once grandad was on his feet again, and feeling better.

'Cruel woman.' Ross's smile belied his words. 'How can you behave so coldly towards me after I've wined and dined you?' His lips brushed her cheek, trailing a tantalising path along the line of her jaw and down over the silky column of her throat.

A sweet shiver of sensation rippled through her, sweeping her body with a delicious languor, making her toes curl and filling her with a strange longing for…for what? His kisses? He was making it hard to resist, so very hard…

Pebbles crunched underfoot as someone walked along the winding path towards them. She pulled a deep breath of air into her lungs and straightened, pushing Ross away gently with the flat of her hand.

'Heather—' He was serious now—the intimate teasing dissolved, replaced by a firmer intent.

She kept her palm in place, though, resisting him—warding him off—then turned to see who it was approaching.

James looked at them guardedly. 'Am I interrupting something?'

She shook her head and said fiercely, 'No.'

'Yes.' Ross's tone was emphatic and rueful at the same time, and James grinned.

'Sorry. It's just that I think Grandad's tiring a bit, and I wondered if we should take him home. He's had a good time, but his breathing's not so great and he could do with an early night. I could go with him, if you want to stay.'

She was instantly alert. 'No. I'll come with you.' She got to her feet, concerned and a little flustered, and brushed herself down while Ross gathered up their discarded plates and took them over to a table nearby.

James murmured softly, 'I guess Martyn has competition. The doctor's OK, I like him.'

'It isn't like that,' Heather protested under her breath. 'We're neither of us thinking about getting involved—we work together, that's all.' She stopped, aware that she was talking too fast, protesting too much and probably giving off mixed signals. 'I must go and check on Grandad. It's time we were leaving, anyway.'

They gave Grandad painkillers for the discomfort in his chest and settled him comfortably in the car. By the time they arrived home some of the pain had eased, and he went off to bed, propped up with pillows to reduce some of the strain on his heart. Heather looked at him as he dozed, and bit her lip. He was frail, and so precious to her, and she was terribly afraid that soon they might lose him.

James put an arm around her shoulders, sensing her distress. 'I'm glad I came over here,' he said quietly. 'Thanks for letting me know how he was. I'll try and get over again...' He didn't say any more, but they both knew what he had been thinking. Before it's too late...

Over the following week Heather forbade Sam to tackle any chores and arranged for someone to stay with him while she had to be at work, and as the days progressed he began to look a little better.

At the surgery she read the lab report on the baby with enteritis, and phoned the mother to tell her that nothing serious had been found.

'He's doing better now, anyway,' the mother told her. 'At least he's not losing weight any longer, and the diarrhoea seems to be clearing up.'

The test results for Richard Stanway were not so good, though, and Heather pointed them out to Ross. 'White cell group HLA B27. It's definitely ankylosing spondylitis, poor man. Until the consultant gets his condition stabilised he's going to need a lot of support. His family ought to know.'

'We can't tell them,' Ross said firmly. 'He has a right to confidentiality. If he doesn't want them to be told, we have to abide by his decision.'

'But you know his circumstances—he's alone, struggling to make a living—he needs their help,' she persisted. 'We should try to do something.'

He stayed adamant. 'There's nothing we can do without his permission.'

Heather's frustration rose, her fingers tightening into fists at her sides. 'But he's not happy the way things are—I know he isn't. Underneath that practical façade he's miserable—I can feel it. There ought to be some way—'

'You can't live his life for him, Heather,' he cut in briskly. 'He's of age and able to make his own decisions—leave it at that.'

'Don't you care? Don't you have any feelings about his situation?'

His mouth tightened. 'Of course I care—but there are times when you have to simply do your job and stand back and let people get on with their lives. You can't take on everybody's problems or you'll be weighed down.' He glanced at his watch. 'I have to go. I'll be late for my clinic.'

She stared angrily after him, then pulled herself together and marched off to her own room. Her own surgery was due to start, but she needed a minute or two before she could bring herself to ring the bell for the first patient.

After that things went on at a fairly even pace. She dealt with the usual minor ailments, aches and pains and summer colds that had turned to chesty coughs. Then she glanced at her next patient's notes and saw that Louise had booked in for an antenatal check.

'I couldn't get to the clinic,' Louise apologised. 'I hope it's all right for me to see you at a normal surgery.'

'Of course. It's just that antenatal checks usually take a little longer than the normal appointments—that's why we book them separately. How are you feeling?'

Louise rested her hands on her abdomen. 'Tired. Carrying this around for six and a half months doesn't help.' It was an heartfelt announcement, made with a grin, and Heather responded with a smile.

'Are you finding time to put your feet up each day for half an hour or so?'

Louise lifted her brows. 'You're joking, aren't you? With Ben at home? When he's at playschool I get on with the housework, and the rest of the time I'm run ragged. There's so much to do, getting the house right for this one...' She patted her bump again affectionately. 'I've only just started on the nursery.'

Heather examined her, checking her weight and listening to the baby's heartbeat. 'That seems fine. Your blood pressure's a little high, but nothing to worry about. You really should try to get some rest, though. You're also slightly anaemic so I'll give you some iron tablets.'

She watched Louise go from the room and rang for her last patient of the afternoon. In the cool light of day Kevin Fraser looked bigger than she remembered, but there was still the faint smell of alcohol on his breath. He seemed unsteady on his feet, and caught the chair with his foot as he came into the room. He sat down and she saw that his colour was sallow and noted that he seemed to be short of breath.

'What can I do for you?'

'It's this guts ache,' he said bluntly. 'Can't face food these days. Always feeling sick, like.'

'I'd better examine you,' Heather told him. 'Would you undo your shirt and lie down on the couch?'

'There's no call for that, is there? I just need some of the white medicine I had once before. That'll do the trick.'

'Possibly. But I need to examine you, all the same. Whereabouts are you getting the pain?'

He grudgingly climbed onto the couch and answered her questions with brief, grunted replies, although when she asked him about his alcohol consumption he became defensive.

'Ain't nothing wrong with having a glass or two,' he said sharply, his voice rising a notch.

'None at all,' Heather agreed, 'if it is just one or two, but I think your problem is caused by rather more than that. I suspect you're anaemic, but I'll need to do blood and urine tests—'

He rolled off the couch and knocked her hand away. 'None of that. I ain't having none of it. I told you—all that's wrong with me is the belly ache. It's the wife's fault—what with her going on about the bills, as if talking about it's going to make 'em disappear. And Natalie getting herself knocked up... I have to have a drink to shut it all out.'

Heather took a deep breath and tried again. 'The thing is, Mr Fraser, your liver probably isn't efficient as it should be, and you need to pay attention to your diet. Eat more protein and make sure you get enough vitamins in your food. I can give you tablets to reduce the fluid build-up that's causing your breathlessness but, basically, I don't think your condition is going to get any better while you continue to drink.'

He pushed her to one side and she fell back, banging into the side of the couch. 'It ain't the drink.' He was angry now, a vein throbbing in his temple. 'Damn quacks—you're all the same. Telling me what to do, how to live my life.' His voice was getting louder.

'Getting the wife to think it's all my fault. I know she came to see you. Well, she won't no more. Spouting our business to all and sundry, encouraging Natalie to keep the baby—more trouble—who's going to look after it? Not me and the wife. She should have got rid of it—'

'Mr Fraser—' His arm swung out and knocked her away, hurling her against the wall so that she cracked her head on the bookshelf.

'Out of the way. I ain't staying here. Keep your medicine—never worked anyway.'

He pulled open the door and slammed it back on its hinges so that it ricocheted against the filing cabinet with a clatter. Dazed, and conscious of a throbbing pain at her temple, Heather steadied herself against the wall and was vaguely aware of Ross, coming into the room.

Kevin Fraser shouldered his way past him, and there was a brief altercation in the corridor as Ross swung round after him. Ross's voice was low, but firm and edged with anger, and it cut right across Kevin's ranting. Heather didn't hear much of what was said, but she caught the sound of the heavy front door of the surgery being banged shut and then the sound of footsteps, coming back this way.

She blinked, trying to clear the haziness from her head.

'Are you all right?' Ross asked, his voice laced with concern. 'You're as white as a sheet. What happened?'

'I'm OK. I fell against something and banged my head.'

His hand cupped her chin, turning her head so he could assess the damage. 'You're bleeding,' he said. 'The man's a menace.'

'I— He…didn't want to know…' she said shakily, as the impact of what had happened began to make inroads on her mind. 'He... I felt so helpless...useless...' her voice trailed away.

Ross put his arms around her and cradled her, and she felt his reassuring strength seep into her, shoring her up. Until then she hadn't realised just how much the incident had shaken her, but now she started to tremble as the aftermath hit her. Her cheek rested against his chest and the steady thud of his heart comforted her.

'Poor love. Hold onto me. He's gone now, you're safe, I've got you.' His hands stroked her gently, calming her.

'He wouldn't let me do any tests. He was so angry— he didn't even stay for a prescription. Ross, I'm not used to feeling this way—so weak. It isn't like me.' She felt guilty, ashamed of her reaction.

'You've had a shock. It's not surprising that you feel this way. He'd been drinking—you didn't stand a chance,' Ross said fiercely. 'You shouldn't have had to deal with him.'

His fingers smoothed her hair, and the tender caress was her undoing. She lifted her face to him. 'You must think I'm a feeble idiot. I've only been here five minutes and this happens. What kind of doctor am I?'

'No, don't say that. You're strong—you've been through a lot lately, with the move down here and the worry about Sam. I'm proud of the way you've coped.' He smiled down at her, and the warmth in his expression melted the cold in her bones. His fingers spread through the silk of her hair, drawing it back from her face, and he tilted her head so that he could gaze down at her. 'My poor girl...' His glance dropped to the fullness of her mouth.

'Heather,' he murmured, and then his head lowered so that his lips were a mere breath away from hers. He took in a ragged breath. 'I've been wanting to do this for such a long time...'

His lips brushed hers, warm and firm, in a tantalising caress that had her mouth parting with tremulous longing. The kiss deepened and he drew her closer to him so that her breasts were softly crushed against the warmth of his chest, and his hands stroked her, gliding over the indentations of her spine to settle satisfyingly around her. His mouth trailed over her cheek and slid down to press gentle kisses on the slope of her throat. She closed her eyes to savour the moment.

Her fingers explored the line of his ribs beneath the light material of his jacket, tracing an upward path to the broad sweep of his shoulders. Her lashes flickered against the cotton of his shirt and she looked up, her gaze dreamily following the line of his collar. Then she gave a soft gasp as she saw the traces of blood there.

'Ross—your shirt. I've ruined it.'

'It doesn't matter,' he murmured, his fingers tightening briefly on her to stop her from pulling away. Then he looked at her properly and said in a roughened voice. 'Oh, Lord, what am I doing? You're hurt...'

He led her over to a chair and sat her down. 'Stay there, and I'll see to that cut.'

'There's no need—'

But he was already moving away, collecting up what he needed, and she couldn't find the strength to argue. His kisses had confused her, made her forget everything for a while, and now that he had gone from her she felt cold again and isolated.

'It isn't too bad,' he said when he had cleaned the area, 'but it needs a couple of butterfly plasters to pull it together. There won't be any scar and, anyway, your hair should hide it.'

'I'm not worried about that. If I'd been more alert I might have been quicker to realise what was happening. I could perhaps have staved off his outburst, done something—'

'Fraser's a drunk, an alcoholic. He's unpredictable, and you shouldn't have been the one to see him. He usually comes to me, but there must have been a glitch in the appointments system. I'll make sure it doesn't happen again.'

'Are you saying that I shouldn't treat him—that there are patients only you can deal with?' She shook her head. 'That isn't right, and you know it.'

'It's the way it's going to be,' he said crisply. 'Either I deal with him or he goes to a different practice. I'm not risking you being hurt again.' He tested the edges of the wound. 'Keep still now.'

'That's ridiculous,' she said curtly. 'You can't make decrees like that in this day and age. A doctor treats patients of all kinds. There are no dividing lines.'

His mouth firmed. 'There are in this instance. Either you abide by what I say or he goes elsewhere. That's the way it's going to be, Heather, whether you like it or not.' He fixed the last butterfly plaster in place.

She scowled at him. 'What happened to democracy? You can't just override my opinions like that.'

'In this instance, I can and I will,' he responded without rancour. 'For better or worse, I'm in charge here and I make the final decisions. I dare say you'll get used to it in time.'

'Don't count on it,' she said tersely, getting to her feet and moving over to the door. 'I doubt very much if I'll be around long enough for that to happen.'

CHAPTER SEVEN

IT WAS just as well she had come to her senses, Heather told herself as the days passed. She had been trying to get the balance right before Ross came bursting into her life, before his easy charm had threatened to topple her carefully ordered existence.

Like Grandad had said, Ross liked to have his own way and she couldn't let herself be drawn to someone who completely disregarded her opinions. She'd had enough of that from her father. It was best that they simply worked together—there wasn't room in her life for anything more.

She was in the same frame of mind when he arrived at the cottage on the following Saturday to see Sam.

'I think we should give him something to improve his heartbeat,' she told him. 'And if he tells you he's feeling better and that he's ready to tackle some of the jobs in the garden—put him straight,' she told him with a rasp. 'It's all I can do to keep him from getting the spade out. He says it's not a woman's job... Honestly, sometimes I despair! I've had to hide the key to the shed.'

'I'll do my best.' Ross grinned and went through to the living room. Heather finished clearing the kitchen, and was putting the teatowel back on the rail when he came into the room again.

'I've given him a prescription, as you suggested, and some antibiotics for the cough. It'll make him feel more comfortable. He's going to rest for a while now.'

His mobile phone started to ring, and he went to answer it.

'Hello, Mrs Fraser, Dr Kennedy here. No, she's not

on duty today, though I can have a word with her, if you like. What's the problem?' There was a pause. He frowned, then jotted a few notes down on a pad that he took from his jacket pocket. 'How far along is her pregnancy? About nine weeks? OK, I'll come over there now.'

He cut the call, and Heather lifted a questioning brow. 'Trouble?'

'Natalie Fraser. Something's gone wrong with the pregnancy, from what I can gather.' He checked his notes. 'This isn't the family address—'

'No. She went to live with her boyfriend. Poor girl, she's had a lot to contend with lately, and now this.'

'Do you want to come along with me? I expect she'd prefer to see you.'

'Yes, I do. Thanks. I'll just get my bag.' She went to tell her grandfather what was happening and make sure he was all right, and then she joined Ross in his car.

The journey didn't take long and they didn't talk much on the way, except to go over Sam's treatment.

Mrs Fraser let them into the flat. 'Oh, Dr Brooks, Natalie will be glad you came along. You've been kind to her. Her boyfriend's out at work today and she's a bit tearful.'

Natalie was in bed, looking very pale and frightened and in obvious pain. Heather went over to her, while Ross spoke quietly to Mrs Fraser at one side of the room.

'I'm so scared, Doctor. Something's really wrong,' Natalie cried, tears falling down her cheeks. 'I know it is—and it hurts so much.'

'Let me take a look,' Heather said. 'I'll be as gentle as I can. Whereabouts is the pain?'

Natalie put a hand to one side of her navel, and Heather carefully examined her.

'There's some swelling here,' she murmured. 'Is the pain there all the time, or does it go away at all?'

'It's there all the time. It's been coming on for a week or so now.'

'Have you had any bleeding at all?'

Natalie nodded miserably. 'Some. Off and on. Not much, though.'

Heather straightened the bedclothes. 'Just rest quietly for a minute while I go and wash my hands, and I'll come back and talk to you.'

She rinsed her hands in the bathroom, and Ross said in an undertone, 'What do you think? Ectopic?'

'That would be my guess. She'll need to go to hospital. I'll tell her—will you talk to her mother?'

'I'll do that. I'll give the hospital a ring and call an ambulance as soon as you've explained things.'

Heather went back to Natalie, who was struggling to sit up in bed. 'Lie back, Natalie,' Heather said. 'Take things easy.'

'What is it?' the girl asked, distressed. 'What's happening to me? Am I going to lose the baby?'

Heather said carefully, 'I think what's happened is that the embryo is developing in the Fallopian tube instead of in the womb, where it should be.'

'Is that bad?' Natalie asked warily, and wiped her damp face with the back of her hand.

'It's not good,' Heather said bluntly. 'It means that you'll need to go into hospital so that they can do tests to find out exactly what's going on.'

'Can't I stay here?'

'No, I'm sorry, Natalie.' The girl began to cry again, and Heather said gently, 'It will be much safer for you in the hospital where you can be looked after properly.'

Ross came and held the girl's hand. 'She's right, you know. You need the proper attention that we can't give you here.'

'And if it is in the Fallopian tube? What then?'

'Then I'm afraid you'll need an operation to remove

the embryo from the tube and repair the damage. But first we need to get to you to the hospital so that they can take care of you.'

Mrs Fraser came to the bedside. 'I'll come with you, Natalie, and I'll ring Mick at work and let him know what's happening. Dry your eyes, love, and I'll get your things together.'

Natalie screwed up her face and buried her head in her hands. 'This is just what Dad wanted, isn't it? It's all going his way.'

Her mother put her arms around her and held her tight, while Natalie's shoulders heaved and she sobbed noisily. Heather's heart twisted in sympathy. Maybe the girl's life had been messed up and the prospect of a baby would probably have made things even more difficult, but this terrible event didn't do anything to dampen any of those feelings that Natalie had already formed for the life within her.

The ambulance arrived a few minutes later, and by then Natalie was calm enough to be settled into it.

Ross spoke to Mrs Fraser as she was preparing to climb in after her daughter. 'Tell her to come to the surgery when this is all over and she's feeling a bit better. There are bound to be questions she wants to ask. We'll do what we can to explain things and put her mind at rest.'

'I'll tell her. Thanks.' Mrs Fraser hesitated, then said, 'I wanted to apologise to the both of you for the way my husband acted the other day. I'm sorry. I know how he gets, and there's no reasoning with him. He needs help but he won't accept it, and he gets everyone's back up the way he goes on. I'm really sorry.'

'It's all right, Mrs Fraser,' Heather said. 'Don't worry about it. Just take care of yourself and Natalie.'

They watched the ambulance move away, then Ross turned to look at her and said softly, 'Come on, I'll take you home. I'd stay with you and Sam for a while but I've two more calls to make before I'm through.'

'Thanks for letting me come with you on this one,' Heather said. 'I wish I'd been able to do more to help. She looked so young and vulnerable.' She made a grimace, sadness creeping into her eyes.

'You're just a softy, really, aren't you?' he murmured, putting an arm around her and giving her a squeeze. 'But, like I said before, you can't take on everyone's problems. It's too wearing. What you need is to have a day out somewhere, a chance to put work behind you for a while. You haven't had a break yet this summer, and you need something different and completely relaxing.'

She couldn't envisage anything right then. 'I'm perfectly happy as I am, thanks.'

He shook his head. 'I'm being serious. A day out on a canal boat, maybe, cruising the waterways. Can you imagine it? Nothing but peace and quiet, the sound of water lapping at the sides of the boat…the sun warming you as you sip a glass of chilled wine.'

'Mmm. Sounds heavenly. But not possible. Not with Grandad the way he is. I don't think he would want to go, and I can't leave him.'

'We'll try to persuade him to come along. It would be a change for him. He can sit in a deckchair and watch the world go by.'

She smiled faintly at that. It wasn't very likely that Ross was being serious—what did either of them know about canal boats? It was just a fanciful whim and he would have forgotten about it by tomorrow.

He went into the cottage with her to check the addresses of his next two calls. Grandad had been dozing, but he came awake as they arrived home and, to Heather's surprise, Ross put the suggestion of a day out to him there and then.

'That's a lovely idea,' Grandad said, and coughed chestily, but his eyes were twinkling with a return of his former self. 'Sounds a real treat. You go ahead and book the boat for the day, lad. When were you thinking of setting out?'

Ross glanced at Heather. 'Is tomorrow all right with you? We've locum cover for the day so there'll be no problem on that score.'

'Of course it's fine with Heather,' Sam put in cheerfully. 'It's high time she had a day out and got some fresh air in her lungs.'

Between the pair of them she was left with little choice but to agree or to be thought a spoilsport, but she did think it sounded good so in the end she gave in gracefully.

'Do I need to pack a hamper?'

'No, don't bother. We'll tie up at a pub for lunch.'

Sunday dawned and Heather thought perhaps the whole idea would fall through because Ross couldn't get a booking, but he arrived with Toby soon after they had finished breakfast, humming softly and good-humouredly to himself.

'All ready to go?' he queried with a smile. 'Do you mind if Toby comes with us? I don't like leaving him for that long—and he'll be as good as gold.'

'I don't mind at all. I'll just fetch a jacket in case the weather turns breezy,' Heather said. 'What about you, Grandad? Is there anything you want to take? A book, perhaps, or the paper?'

'No, lass. I shan't be needing anything. I'm staying here and spending the day with Frank and Harry. They're bringing the dominoes with them and a pack of cards, and Harry's wife's making up some food for us. She's off to her sister's for the day. I'll be just fine. You go off and have fun.'

Heather's mouth dropped open. 'Grandad, you agreed to come with us on the boat—'

'No, I didn't, love. I said it was a good idea, and it is. It's time you two young things had a chance to relax and be on your own. You and Ross should get out more. You don't need me along.'

'But, Grandad—' She broke off as the front doorbell sounded, and she went to answer it, opening the door to Sam's friends.

'Are we too early?'

'Right on time,' Grandad called out. 'Come on in.'

Ross chuckled as Heather showed them into the kitchen and stood, watching the trio, a dazed expression on her face.

'You go off and have fun. I'm sorry I tricked you but I'll be fine, love. Go and enjoy yourself.'

'He's a wily old soul, isn't he?' Ross murmured.

'You can say that again!' She waggled her finger at her grandfather, laughing in spite of herself. 'I'll never trust you again, you mischievous old devil. You'd better behave, you hear? And make sure you page me if you need me.'

'And you two will stay with him till we get back, won't you?' Ross asked Frank and Harry.

They promised faithfully, and Ross took Heather's arm and ushered her out to his car before she could administer any more dire warnings. She looked back towards the house, wondering if she was doing the right thing. Would they know what to do if anything happened?

'Leave them to it,' Ross said. 'They'll be fine.' Toby jumped into the back of the car and settled himself to look out of the window.

'I wish I could be as sure,' she muttered, half cross, half amused. 'The old devil! Do you know, the way he's behaving lately it's almost as though he wants us to get together.'

Ross shot her an oblique glance as he set the car in motion. His mouth twitched. 'I had that feeling too. Something about the way he looked at us. I think he's decided we make a good pair and he's trying to give us a bit of a push.'

Heather threw her head back and chuckled. 'At least he's happy, I suppose, and that's the main thing.'

'And he's made you laugh. That's a bonus in itself. Now, sit back and enjoy the day.'

They reached the mooring and found their boat, a shiny red and green canal barge with brightly painted canal buckets on top and signs along the sides of the boat, decorated with flowers and showing the name, MARYLOU.

'I hope you know how to drive that thing,' she said. 'Or, at least, that we're insured while we're on it!'

'Worry, worry. Have you no faith?' Ross chided with a grin. 'Of course I know how to drive it. I've spent enough Sunday lunches over a pint at the Sorrel Lock, watching people negotiate the waters. How difficult can it be?'

He must have seen the look of horror that came over her face because he laughed and took pity on her. 'Of course I've done it before, idiot. Do you really think I'd risk taking you out for the day if I didn't have a clue? Climb on board and try not to look so panic-stricken. You'll be quite safe with me.' Then his eyes took on a wicked glitter and he added in an undertone, 'As long as you want to be safe, that is.'

She wasn't going to take him up on that. Just the thought of being alone with him for the next few hours was doing strange things to the rhythm of her pulse.

'Let's just concentrate on keeping afloat, shall we?' Everything about him put her senses on alert, his easy manner, the way he looked—tall, strong, so definitely male in a T-shirt that accentuated his broad shoulders and contrasted with his lightly tanned skin and the equally snug-fitting jeans that clung to his long, muscular legs. She swallowed quickly and turned her gaze away from him, following Toby onto the deck.

The dog bounded down the stairway into the galley, and she peered down the steps after him. It was neat down there, a compact little kitchen which gave way to the sitting area, with curtained windows for looking out on the scene. Toby sniffed around, then came back up on deck.

'Do you want to go down and take a look around?' Ross was busy, starting up the engine, and she shook her head.

'I'd prefer it up here for now. It's going to be a beautiful day, just the right amount of breeze. Can I give you a hand with anything?'

'You could coil up that rope and stow it out of the way,' he said, indicating the rope with a sideways jerk of his head and keeping his eyes on the way ahead.

They left the mooring pond behind and glided through countryside, disturbing little families of waterfowl along the route. Heather smiled as she watched the ducklings swim after their parents or dive for food and surface again, swishing their bodies to shake off the water.

She stood beside Ross and he put an arm around her shoulder, pointing out the watermill in the distance and the old red brick farmhouse where sheep grazed in the meadow beyond. They travelled for miles, slowly and steadily, and she needn't have worried about his handling of the boat. He manoeuvred it perfectly.

'It's so lovely out here.' Heather sighed contentedly. 'I think I could take to this life.' They passed through acres of land where fields stretched on either side and through serene places where the waterway widened and

trees spread their branches out over the water and the
sunlight dappled the surface. At intervals they had to
stop and negotiate the lock gates, waiting for the water
to reach the right level before they could go on. She
watched him working the gates, his muscles taut, his
whole body radiating lithe energy, and heat flamed inside her.

'We'll pull in downstream and stop at the next lock
for lunch,' Ross said. 'They serve delicious food at the
pub, and there's usually plenty of room to sit outside.'

It was the middle of the day, and a lot of people had
had the same thought, but they arrived early enough to
find a bench table free close to the water's edge. Toby
ran around excitedly for a while, rushing backwards and
forwards along the path—enjoying the freedom—but
when Ross called he came to his side and dropped, panting, on the grass. They ordered cheese salad and French
fries, with crusty rolls and butter, and cold cider to wash
it down. When the food arrived she saw that there was
a basket of fries for Toby.

Heather laughed as he tucked in. 'I can't believe I was
scared of him that day,' she murmured, looking down at
his smooth black head. 'He's just a big, soft, boisterous
child at heart.'

'He thinks he's part of the family, really. When I eat
he eats. When Ben plays football he plays football.
You're right. He's soft and he's totally loyal—he'd pro-
tect any of us the instant there was any danger. I had
him as a pup from a litter my mother supervised into the
world.'

'She's a vet?'

'Yes, she adores animals. Dad's a doctor, retired now,
but he keeps his hand in, doing the odd afternoon filling
in when anyone's sick.'

'Is that why you went in for medicine—because of
the family tradition?'

'It's in the blood, I think. I never wanted to do anything else. What about you? What made you decide—other than not wanting to join the family firm?'

She swallowed her drink and put the glass down on the table. 'Several things, I suppose. The usual, wanting to do something to help other people, and to do something that mattered—that made a difference. A friend of mine was taken ill when I was very young at primary school. She had a nut allergy and she ate something, without realising that nuts were part of the ingredients—a biscuit, I think. The reaction was awful. She couldn't breathe and went into a state of collapse. Luckily, her parents knew about the allergy, and the staff were prepared. The headmistress gave her an injection, and she stabilised enough for them to get her to hospital. She recovered, and I thought how wonderful it was to have the knowledge and the skill to make such a difference—to save a life.'

They stayed at the pub for an hour or so, enjoying the heat of the day, until Toby became restless and they took him for a walk along the tow-path, taking a route through the fields.

They lingered at a stile and Heather looked over to the trees and watched the birds lazily circle and call to each other.

'This has been a beautiful summer,' she murmured. 'I can't remember the last time I felt so…complete. Back home, it all seems to be work and rush and it's all somehow very serious. But here, somehow, it's different. There's something about the place…'

'Perhaps you belong here,' Ross said quietly. 'Maybe you should forget about going back home. Stay here and start putting down roots.'

'Stay here?' she echoed. 'I can't…'

'Why not? Your grandfather needs you for longer than a few more weeks. You'll face this decision again, you know. You won't be able to escape it.' He moved closer and reached for her, his hands drawing her to him. 'You could settle here, if you wanted to. What's so important back home?'

She didn't answer, but her eyes were troubled, and he murmured softly, 'You're happy here, you've lost the tense look that you had when you first came—can't I persuade you to stay?' His finger traced the line of her cheek and strayed to brush the softness of her mouth, outlining its gentle curve and leaving a trail of heat in its wake. Then, when she was still mesmerised by that gentle caress, he touched her mouth with his own and she was lost in a world of tender passion and heady intoxication, as though she'd sipped a delicious, sweet wine that filled her veins with liquid fire.

Her lips parted, opening to the warmth of his kiss, and her breath snagged in her throat as she felt the ragged need in him and an answering throb of response melted her limbs. His hands were moving over her as though he would memorise every plane and every curve, and when his fingers cupped the soft swell of her breast with tender possession she felt as though she was drowning in a tide of wild, hot sensation.

'You feel so good,' he muttered thickly. 'I can't help myself when I'm with you like this. I want more, much more.' With his other hand he urged her closer, and she groaned huskily as her thighs tangled with his and he moved against her, rocking gently.

An ache of desire shuddered through her as her body took up the undulating rhythm. Her fingers curled into the rippling muscles of his shoulders, and she pressed her mouth to the soft skin at the base of his throat.

'Ah, Heather...' he muttered, his voice roughened with passion, 'let me love you...'

She was sorely tempted. Their bodies might have been made for each other they fitted together with such gratifying ease, such pleasurable intimacy, and she had never been so feverishly aware of the clamour of her senses, urging her to throw caution to the wind.

'Ross, I…' It was the gentle nuzzle of silk against her leg that dissolved the mist and brought her back to reality with a bump. She frowned, and twisted around to see what was happening. Toby nudged her again.

'I'd almost forgotten about him,' Ross admitted with a rueful grimace. 'About everything, really—except being here with you. This is no place for what I had in mind.'

'It's just as well he reminded us,' Heather said huskily, her head clearing rapidly now. What had she been thinking of, kissing him like that? What had happened to all her plans to keep things on a level plain? 'Ross, this was all a mistake. It should never have happened.'

'You're right, this is no place to be making love to you—out in the open in broad daylight where anyone might have come along. Our reputations could have been shredded in an instant.' There was a gleam in his eye, but Heather bit her lip and shook her head.

'No… I mean it… I don't know why I let it happen. Let's just stay friends, Ross, and forget about it…'

He was busy picking up Toby's lead and bringing him to heel, but he stopped and looked at her. 'Do you really believe you can turn your emotions on and off, like flicking a switch? What's behind this sudden change of heart?'

How could she begin to explain when she was in a state of utter confusion? She ran her hands over her jeans while she tried to find the right words, and he waited, watching her through narrowed eyes.

'We work together,' she said at last, 'and maybe we should leave it at that. I'll be going back home sooner or later, and it wouldn't do for us to get involved. You have your life here, and I have one waiting for me back home, one that I've built up over the years. I've been given the chance of a place in a city practice, and it would be sensible to accept it. I know the partners, and I get on well with them. The prospects are good. Besides that, my friends are all back there, the people I grew up with, along with James and my father.'

His expression was cynical. 'Do you really think you'd be happy, going back to town life? You're kidding yourself. What's really at the back of all this?'

'It's what I'm used to, what I've grown up with. All my training has been centred on busy health centres and local hospitals.'

'That doesn't mean you can't try something else.'

'Look, I don't want to talk about it any more,' she said firmly. 'We should be starting back. Let's not spoil the day by arguing.'

He shrugged. 'If that's how you want it that's fine by me, but you won't be able to run away for ever, you know. Some time soon you're going to have to think seriously about whether you're making the right decision.'

They started back along the path to where the boat was moored and neither of them brought up the subject again, but instead came to an uneasy truce. Heather tried not to think about the moments they'd shared by the stile in the warmth of the sun. It was just her hormones, acting up, she told herself crossly. She was away from home and thrown into his company, and it was small wonder that her nerves were stretched.

Coming here, to the country, was meant to be a break, a chance to do some thinking and get herself back on an even keel, and all that had happened was that Ross had turned up and complicated things even more.

It was a tense journey back. They reached home around teatime, and Ross insisted on coming into the house with her to see how Grandad had fared during the day.

They were both shocked when Frank confronted them in the living room, his weathered face lined with anxiety.

'He had a funny turn just a few minutes ago,' he reported quickly. 'We got him upstairs to bed between us, and we were just wondering whether to page you or call the locum out. I wasn't sure what to do. It might just be that he needs to rest a bit. I thought he was overdoing things, dragging the barbecue and the charcoal out of the shed.'

Heather felt the blood drain from her face, but she managed to call up her resources and grab her medical bag before she headed for the stairs. Ross was close behind her. She took a moment to compose herself outside Grandad's room, then she opened the door quietly and went to his bedside.

His eyelids came open as they approached, and he smiled at her, his glance going to Ross who came and stood beside her. 'Did you two have a good day?'

'It was lovely,' Heather told him, arranging his pillows so that he was more comfortable.

'Good.' He looked at Ross and said oddly, 'I knew she'd be all right with you.'

He sounded breathless, and Heather asked quietly, 'Are you in any pain?'

He nodded, and she poured him a drink and handed him his tablets.

'Thanks, love. Don't look so worried.' He paused to swallow them and get his breath back. 'I'm not afraid, you know. Sooner or later I'll meet up with my Jenny again. I just need to see you settled.'

Heather laid a hand on his shoulder, kneading it gently. 'You should try to rest, Grandad,' she said in a choked voice. 'I knew I shouldn't have left you to your own devices. Trying to set up the barbecue—honestly, you're not to be trusted when my back's turned.'

His mouth lifted at the corners. 'Snitched on me, did they? Wait till I get my strength back.' His voice trailed off weakly, and he closed his eyes, drifting off into a doze. Heather stood and watched him for a minute or two until Ross put an arm around her and led her away.

'He'll sleep for a while,' he murmured. 'At least he's content for now.'

They went downstairs and Ross spoke quietly to Frank and Harry, while Heather put the kettle on. They wouldn't stay, though, and Ross saw them out.

The phone rang, and she went to answer it. Martyn's voice came as a bit of a shock, and she sat down abruptly at the kitchen table.

'Heather—I called earlier but your grandfather said you were out.'

'That's right. How are you—is everything all right?'

'Yes, of course. I finished working my southern section ahead of time, which left me free for the day. I was thinking about you, and wanted to talk. There's been so little chance for us to do that lately, with our working hours clashing. Your grandfather said you were out on a canal boat for the day.

'If I'd known you were going to be free for any length of time we could have arranged to meet. I'd have driven over there, but I thought you had to stay near your grandfather because he was so ill.' His tone reproached her, and added to the guilt she was already feeling for having left Grandad.

She was conscious of Ross, coming back into the room and she waved him over to the coffee-pot. 'Things didn't work out quite as I'd planned,' she said, returning her attention to Martyn. 'He was supposed to have come with us, but—'

'But he didn't, apparently.' He sounded curt, and

Heather felt a little indignant that he hadn't let her finish, but before she could say any more he asked, 'So, who went along on this trip?'

'Dr Kennedy. The man I work with.' She saw Ross add cream to his coffee and test the liquid.

'Just you and him? No one else?'

'No one else. Look, Martyn—'

'You don't have to explain,' he cut in. 'I think I'm beginning to understand now why you've been so keen to stay on at your grandfather's place. I'd assumed it was because he was ill, but I see things are not quite what they seemed.'

'He *is* ill. Martyn, you're not seeing this from my point of view. I've told you how things are at the moment—'

'So you have. Where do my feelings come into consideration? Don't you think I've put up with your whims for long enough? We've been together a long time, and I feel I'm entitled to some kind of commitment from you, Heather, some acknowledgement that we might have a future together. But not now, in a telephone conversation, where we can't see each other face to face. We'll talk about it some other time.'

He cut the call, leaving her with the dialling tone and a growing sense of frustration. Was he right? Had she been putting his feelings to one side? But she'd tried to explain how she felt, hadn't she? It was Martyn who kept insisting that they had a future together, even though she had doubts.

Ross pushed a mug of coffee towards her. 'Someone from back home?' One dark eyebrow lifted in query.

'Yes.' She picked up the mug and sipped slowly.

'It didn't sound as though he was very happy with things.'

She glared at him. 'That was supposed to be a private conversation,' she said tersely.

'Then you'd have done better if you'd asked me to leave. As it is, I have a fair idea now about why you suddenly had second thoughts this afternoon about getting involved with me.'

Her fingers clenched on the mug. 'It isn't a question of second thoughts,' she retorted repressively. 'I wasn't thinking at all and that's the crux of the matter. It never should have happened.'

His eyes narrowed on her. 'But it did, Heather, and you can't escape the fact that you kissed me with every bit as much fervour as I kissed you.'

She took in a sharp breath and slammed her mug down on the table, her jaw clenching. 'I told you—it was a mistake. I don't want to talk about it…and I wish you would go now. I can't think straight with Grandad ill in bed.'

His mouth twisted. 'Deny it as much as you like, Heather, but it happened, and now you have to ask yourself why. How much does this man back home mean to you if you can forget him even for an instant and make love with someone else?'

She gasped at that, and stumbled to her feet. 'It wasn't like that,' she said fiercely.

'Wasn't it? If Toby hadn't disturbed us, how far would it have gone?'

'That's unfair,' she muttered shakily, her fingers gripping the edge of the table for support, as if he'd dealt her a body blow.

'It is, isn't it? But life's like that.' His eyes glittered as he raked her taut features. 'Things don't fit neatly into sterile little boxes, much as you might like them to. Think about it. I'll see you at the surgery tomorrow.'

CHAPTER EIGHT

THE week that followed was a busy one, and it helped to keep Heather from dwelling on the tension that existed between her and Ross whenever they came into close contact.

Once or twice she thought Ross might have been about to broach the subject of Martyn with her but they'd been interrupted and, anyway, she didn't want to talk about something which was such a sensitive issue, especially since her mind was in such a whirl. Instead, she stayed remote from him, withdrawn into her own thoughts.

The situation had seemed clear-cut to her before. She needed to be with Grandad, and everything else came second to that. She had been content to put her emotions on a back burner, but now both Ross and Martyn were pushing her to face up to her true feelings.

She didn't want to think about any of it. Nothing was straightforward and simple any more, and it gave her a headache, just thinking about it. Why was everything so difficult for her to deal with? It was far easier to simply concentrate on her work instead. Her patients' problems seemed much easier to solve than her own.

Richard Stanway came to see her one morning, and she studied him thoughtfully as she asked him to take a seat.

'I've had a letter from the consultant at the hospital, Richard, outlining his findings. Did he explain anything to you?'

Richard lowered himself carefully into a chair. 'He

said I'd need to keep going back to the hospital for check-ups. There's a problem with my spine that means I'll need to take tablets for quite some time, and I need to keep the spine mobile. He said swimming was good, and I could use the hospital pool.' Richard paused. 'He asked me if there was anyone in the family with similar symptoms. Why did he want to know that, do you think?'

'You have an illness that is considered to be heredi- tary, Richard,' Heather explained, 'so it's quite likely that if you had a brother or sister they would have had some symptoms.'

He shook his head. 'I don't have any brothers or sis- ters.'

'How are you feeling at the moment?'

'A bit stiff. The early mornings are still bad, but the people at work have been really good to me. They know I'm a bit better later on in the day.'

'I can give you an anti-inflammatory to take over- night, which should help with that,' Heather said, mak- ing out a prescription. 'Painkillers, too. How are you coping otherwise?'

'I get by, I suppose. Does my head in sometimes, but there's not much point in complaining—no one to listen, anyway.' He gave her a wry smile that pinched at her heart. Not to have anyone—that was a terrible thing.

'You still haven't been in touch with your family?'

'No point. My dad never thought much of me. He was always making out I was a disappointment to him.'

Heather was troubled by his acceptance of the situa- tion. 'People change. Couldn't you phone your parents, or write to them? I expect your mother will want to know how you are.'

'Maybe I'll send a card at Christmas.'

That was an awful long way off, Heather thought,

watching him walk slowly from her room. He needed support now.

She cast off her gloomy thoughts as her next patient sat down.

'Hello, Louise,' she said with a smile. 'Antenatal again, is it?'

'Antenatal, yes. I booked your last appointment of the morning so that it wouldn't overlap anyone else's time.'

'How are things? Are you managing to get some rest?'

'I'm in the middle of painting a mural on the nursery wall,' Louise said with a grin. 'Woodland creatures. It's taking an age to get it just right. You'll have to come over and see it when it's finally finished.'

'I'll look forward to it.' She stood up. 'Let's check you over.'

After a few minutes Heather said with a faint frown, 'Your blood pressure's up again, and you've put on a bit more weight than I might have expected. It's hard to tell whether it's due to fluid retention, but your ankles are slightly swollen. I really think you're going to have to rest more, or we'll need to send you to hospital so that they can keep an eye on you. We must get your blood pressure down.'

'Oh, I will try,' Louise promised. 'It's not easy, though.'

'I know, but you have to make a serious effort to relax every day. Eat plenty of protein as well. Meat, fish, cheese, eggs.'

'OK, I'll do my best.'

Heather saw her to the door and went with her towards Reception. She needed to go over her paperwork. Ross was there, checking the post, and she realised it was going to be impossible to find an excuse to slip away and not talk. Louise would think it very odd.

Ross looked at his sister with an affectionate grin. 'How's the bump getting along?'

'Fine, so far. But Heather's been telling me off. Says I have to rest or she's threatened me with hospital. Aagh!' She laughed. 'How am I going to tell Ben that Mummy's having a sit-down when he wants to play cricket in the garden? If his dad was here he'd take him off my hands, but he's away at a conference until tomorrow evening.'

'I could keep Ben with me for the afternoon tomorrow,' Ross suggested.

'Are you sure? Won't you be busy?'

'No problem. I'll pick him up after Saturday morning surgery, if you like. I'll be free by then, but you have to promise me that you'll take things easy.'

That was typical of Ross, Heather thought. He was open and generous, a very caring man.

'You're a treasure,' Louise told him, giving him a hug. 'Ben loves being with you.'

'That's settled, then.' He saw Louise out to her car, and Heather brought her mind back to the sheaf of papers in her tray.

'Anything I should know about?' Ross asked, coming back to find her studying a report. 'Whatever it is, it's made you frown.'

'It's from the hospital. Natalie Fraser's notes.' She scanned the paper. 'Nothing we didn't expect, poor girl. It was definitely an ectopic pregnancy. The blood tests showed less HCG than normal.' Heather pointed to the results that showed the level of the hormone, human chorionic gonadotrophin, which would have been much higher in a pregnancy developing properly within the womb.

'They did an ultrasound and a laparoscopy—the embryo was about to rupture the Fallopian tube.'

'So—did they do a salpingectomy?' Ross queried, and Heather nodded.

'Yes, they had to remove the tube, and the ovary as well, unfortunately.'

'Lucky she had two, then. Presumably, the other one is all right?'

'Yes, it appears so.' Heather put the report to one side. It would have been horrible if a girl as young as Natalie had been condemned to infertility. As it was, they had to hope that any future pregnancy would proceed normally.

Ross glanced at her briefly as she leafed through the rest of her papers.

'How's Sam?'

It was neutral territory, Heather thought, glad that he wasn't referring back to more personal things. At least today they were able to talk in a companionable enough fashion, more the way they used to. She was saddened, though, thinking about Grandad.

'He's improving a little, but he's having a lot of disturbed nights. The problem is that his heart is failing, and all we can do is give him palliative treatment. He ought to be in hospital but he won't hear of it, and I don't really blame him. He wants to be in his own home in familiar surroundings.'

'That's understandable. I could drop by tomorrow afternoon and visit him. Ben will be with me—will that be a problem?'

'I shouldn't think so. I'm expecting James and my young nephew and niece for the day. They'll all be able to play together. We'll keep an eye on Grandad to see that he doesn't get tired.'

They were out in the garden when Ross arrived the next day. Heather and James were tackling the weeds, sprouting in the flowerbeds, while the youngsters, Simon and Charlotte, were telling Grandad all about their outing to the zoo with their mother.

'We saw some penguins,' five-year-old Simon said. 'I nearly fell in the pool and Mummy was cross.'

'I saw a lion when I went with my mum and dad,' Ben joined in. 'He growled and opened his mouth wide and showed all his teeth.'

Heather smiled, listening to the children's tales, then turned to James. 'Didn't you go with them?' she asked.

'I never seem to have the time lately,' he confessed. 'In the end, Laura took them with her sister. She said she was fed up with my excuses, and it was time the kids had a break from my bad temper.'

'Oh, dear. Things aren't getting any better between you two, then?'

'Worse, I'd say,' James admitted shortly. 'I'm always snapping and irritable. I know I'm doing it but it's hard to stop, especially when I'm trying to concentrate on papers I've brought home to work on and the children disrupt things.' He glanced at Ross. 'Sorry you have to hear all this. I don't get much chance to see Heather these days, and all I seem to do is offload my troubles on her.'

'Sometimes talking helps,' Ross said. 'Don't mind me. I can imagine things get difficult for you. Perhaps you need a holiday.'

James gave a wry, bitter-sounding laugh at that. 'Chance would be a fine thing. We're rushed off our feet at work, setting up new branches, and we've had to take on more staff, which means management problems are more urgent. My father says holidays will have to wait until later in the year when things are more settled.'

He finished clearing the patch of garden he was working on and got to his feet, brushing his hands on his trousers.

Ross frowned. 'Can't you insist you have a break now, even if it's just for a week?'

James shook his head. 'Not if I want to be made managing director. My father's always been determined that I should work my way up from the bottom of the heap so that I know every rung of the ladder and there could no backbiting from the workforce. I suppose he's right. Laura gets upset about the slog to the top, though, and she didn't see why we had to do without a break. That's why I have the children. She's had enough and has gone to her mother's.' He glanced at the children who were playing on the lawn.

'For the weekend, you mean?' Heather asked.

James's mouth twisted. 'I hope it's just for the weekend. The mood she was in, it could well be longer.'

He went to wash his hands in the kitchen, and Heather cleared away the garden tools, her expression faintly brooding.

'Are you upset about your brother and his wife?' Ross asked softly. 'Or is it your father's attitude that bothers you?'

Heather turned troubled eyes to him. 'Both, I suppose. I just wonder, sometimes, if any marriage stands a chance. So many couples end up in the divorce courts, and how many of those that don't are really happy?'

'A good number are perfectly content with their lot.'

'And the rest leave behind them a litter of broken homes and unhappy children. It all seems so sad. I don't think I could cope seeing my family life come unglued.'

'Have you been thinking about marriage—to the man back home? What's his name?'

'Martyn. He asked me, yes.'

Ross's eyes narrowed, his mouth making a faintly grim linc. 'But you're not sure? Because you look around and see what might happen?'

'Perhaps. I know what it was like to listen to adults, yelling at each other and saying hurtful things day after day. As a child I sat and wondered why my parents didn't get on, why my father didn't love me, whether my parents stayed together for our sake. I think my father resented us being around. Well—me, anyway. He was OK with James mostly but, then, he was the first born and a boy. All men want a son, don't they?'

'Probably. Have you considered that it isn't the idea of marriage that's wrong, but that Martyn is the wrong man?'

'No one's perfect. I haven't had much reason to think badly of Martyn.'

'That's hardly an answer.' He might have said more, but Ben came up to him at that moment and said, 'Grandad says there's a ball in the shed. Will you play footy with us? Charlotte's just a girl, but she says she wants to play as well.'

'Do you think we should let her, then?' Ross asked, straight-faced.

Ben thought about it, and nodded. 'I think that would be all right.'

'We'd better go and find the ball, then, hadn't we?' Ross said, glancing sideways at Heather and hiding a grin.

She rolled her eyes comically and went over to Grandad, sitting on the bench, and watched the children run over the grass, eagerly kicking the ball and racing about laughing and shouting. They were vying for Ross's attention. He was good with them, and they were happy, brimful of fun.

Her throat constricted, seeing them chuckle and clap their hands with glee. What would her children be like if she ever married? Images of dark-haired, grey-eyed little people swam into her mind. She shook the images away.

'That's what this place needs,' Grandad commented. 'Children. It's a long time since you and James ran about here and wore away that patch of earth under the swing.' He smiled, his eyes glazing over with fond memories.

It was still there, the swing, suspended from the branches of the huge old plum tree at the far side of the lawn, and Heather felt a lump come into her throat, remembering how they used to play.

'Heather fell off it once because I pushed her too hard,' James said, with a rueful smile. 'I thought she was going to cry for hours!'

'They were good times, though,' Heather said, and Grandad nodded.

'Pity your father didn't come to stay and see what it was like to have you all relaxed and happy. He was always a difficult man to know. Convinced that your mother was having a fling and that's why she loved being here.'

'Is that true?' Heather asked, her eyes widening.

James's jaw had dropped open, and Ross, who had come over to take a breather, quirked a brow and sat down on the old stone wall while the children played.

'It's true that he thought that. She was an attractive woman, your mother. You take after her, Heather—same hair colour, same eyes, similar features. Of course, there were men who were drawn to her, for her personality as much as her looks. Like the pharmácist in the village— he's upped and moved away long since—he had a yen for your mother. They were very like-minded, and were always chatting together. Jane was loyal to your father, though. Your nan always said she had a strong sense of what was right and wrong.' He didn't say any more, but watched the children chase each other across the grass. Then he closed his eyes and seemed to doze a little.

Heather hadn't realised she was holding her breath, but now she expelled it slowly and Ross caught her eye. Somehow he must have guessed what she had been thinking. She could read it in his expression, and it struck her that they understood each other well.

She left James talking to Grandad and went to the kitchen to fetch dishes of ice cream for everyone and fill a jug with fruit drink. Ross followed her.

'Anything I can do to help?'

'Thanks. You could put some glasses on the tray.'

He obliged, casting her an oblique glance. 'Were you shocked by that revelation about your mother?'

She thought about it. 'Not shocked because she didn't do anything wrong. Startled, perhaps. When we're young we tend not to think of our parents as having private lives. We either don't think about it at all or imagine that we have a monopoly on their feelings.'

'How do you know she didn't succumb? You said yourself that your parents were always arguing. Isn't it possible that her head was turned?'

Heather collected spoons and added them to the tray. 'I don't think that's what happened. Grandad said she was strong-minded, and I respect his judgement. He's always been able to read people very well.'

'Don't you think she might have grabbed the chance for happiness?' Ross persisted. 'Didn't she deserve it?'

'Yes, she deserved to be happy, but she made her vows in church and I dare say she was determined to stand by them.'

He smiled, satisfied by her answer. He leaned back against the worktop and said carefully, 'Maybe she thought there was something worth holding onto in her marriage?'

Heather was quiet for a moment, thinking it through, then she said softly, 'You could be right. I tend to see things in black and white, but there are all sorts of shades in between, aren't there? While the marriage lasted I think she tried to make it work.'

She hadn't expected his insight into the situation, and it warmed her to know that he understood what she was trying to come to terms with.

'Are you ready to take these outside?' He came around the table and reached for one of the trays, his thigh brushing her side as he stopped beside her. Her whole body came to throbbing life with that brief contact, and he must have been aware of it, too, because he became very still and she thought she heard the swift intake of his breath. She might have misread things, though. He straightened and looked at her, waiting, and she had to drag her thoughts back to what he had said.

'Yes,' she managed. 'I'm ready, except for Grandad's tablets. I'll get them.'

Over the next week or two Heather looked for some change for the better in Grandad's condition, but it was wishful thinking. She was terribly afraid that he was going downhill and it hurt her to see it happening. He never complained, but some nights she got up to give him painkillers and make him more comfortable, and when she woke in the morning she often found she was still sitting in the chair by his bed, his hand clasped in hers.

That was how she had woken this Friday morning when he stirred and she realised with a sense of shock that she must have overslept.

'You'll be late for your visits,' he murmured sleepily. 'I kept you up most of the night. I'm sorry, love.'

'Don't be.' She smiled at him fondly. 'How do you feel?'

'Tired,' he said, and closed his eyes, and she guessed he needed his tablets. She went to get them, and hurried to prepare for the day.

Usually Frank or Harry kept him company while she was away, taking surgery or making her calls, and it helped to know he was with friends. She yawned wearily, checked her messages, then set off for work.

There were more visits than usual and she only had time for a hurried snack with Grandad at lunchtime. He was short of breath and she made him as comfortable as she could before it was time to leave again and start afternoon surgery. It was a long one, with consultations that tended to run on. Natalie Fraser was her last patient of the afternoon.

'How are you feeling?' Heather asked.

The girl looked pale and miserable, and made a grimace. 'So—so. I've started a period and it's hurting a lot, and it's heavier than I'm used to. Does it mean that something's wrong?' She sounded frightened and Heather hastened to reassure her.

'It just means that your womb is getting back to normal. You could try taking a painkiller and lie down with a hot-water bottle—that should make you feel a bit better.'

'I don't think I'll ever feel better.' Natalie's face puckered. 'Sometimes I think I'll have this empty place inside of me for ever. People don't understand. They say it was only a few weeks old, hardly anything, and not even where it should have been—' She broke off and started to cry, and Heather went to her and put a comforting arm around the thin shoulders. Sometimes people meant well, but had no idea how their words could hurt.

'You have a right to grieve, Natalie. Let it out, tell me what you're feeling.'

'It was my baby,' she sobbed quietly. 'We hadn't

planned it, but it happened and I would have taken care of it. One of the doctors at the hospital said we were young and we didn't have much, and perhaps it was for the best, but he didn't know how much I would have loved it. It was part of me, and I wanted to take care of it.'

'Of course you did, Natalie,' Heather murmured. 'I expect he meant well, but he didn't know what it's like to have a child growing inside you or how strong your feelings are.'

'Why couldn't they take it from the tube and put it in my womb? Why did it have to die?' She lifted her tear-streaked face to Heather, her eyes bereft.

'It wouldn't have survived,' she told her sadly. 'There was nothing else they could do, you see, and they had to make sure that you were safe—that's why you had the operation.'

Natalie dashed the tears away with her fingers, and Heather pushed a box of tissues towards her so that she could blow her nose.

When she had herself together again, Natalie asked, 'Will I be able to have a child at all? Will the same thing happen again?'

'We can't say for certain, but you still have another ovary and another healthy Fallopian tube so you should be able to conceive. You should wait a while before trying, though. At least three cycles, I'd say. If you do think that you're pregnant, come and see us at the surgery as soon as possible so that we can arrange for an early scan to make sure that everything's going ahead properly.'

'I will.' Natalie stood up and went to the door. 'Thanks for listening. I felt so alone, as though no one understood. Mum tried to help me, but she has her own problems.'

'I know. If you need to talk, or if you're worried about anything, come and see me again.'

Heather felt drained after she had gone. It was probably the combination of Natalie's grief and her own disturbed nights, but her head was beginning to throb and she felt incredibly weary. She wanted to go home and go to bed but she had to stay alert, be on her guard for any change in Grandad's condition.

Ross had finished his calls for the day, and met her at the door as she was preparing to leave. He looked at her closely.

'Is everything all right, Heather?'

'Fine,' she said shortly, and his brows drew together.

'No problems in surgery?'

'None. Everything went smoothly.'

'Sure?'

Her brittle control snapped. 'What is this—an inquisition? I said everything was fine and I meant it.'

'I don't believe you,' he said bluntly. 'You're very pale and, frankly, you look as though you've been through a wringer.'

'I'm sorry you don't like the way I look,' she said through stiff lips, 'but I'm perfectly all right, and I'd like to go home now—if you would kindly move out of the way of the door.' She knew she was being unfair, but she didn't have it in her to explain things right now.

He stared at her silently for a moment, as though he was debating with himself over something, but then he moved to one side, holding open the door to let her through.

Grandad was in the living room, watching television with Harry, when she arrived home, and she could see straight away that there was no improvement on the morning. He was still breathless and weak, but he gave her a cheerful smile and squeezed her hand as she kissed him.

She saw Harry out, and she had turned her mind to the problem of tackling some of the chores when there was a knock on the kitchen door.

Ross was waiting outside, two carriers in his hands giving off delicious smells.

'I dropped in at the Chinese take-away,' he explained. 'You were exhausted, and I thought it might help if you didn't have to cook this evening.'

She stared at him, taking in the sight of him standing there, and a lump came into her throat. 'That was a wonderful thought.' The smell of the food teased her nostrils, and she opened the door wider. 'Come on in before it gets cold. I'll put some plates under the grill to warm.'

'Do you mind if I join you? Only—'

'Of course you'll join us. Oh, Ross, I'm sorry I was such a grouse earlier. I was tired, that's all, and—'

'And worried about Sam. I know, I guessed as much. I thought maybe I could help.'

She pulled him into the kitchen and scarcely gave him a second to put the bags down on the table before she slid her arms around him and rested her head on his chest. 'You're such a lovely, lovely man. I don't deserve to have you help me out after the way I treated you.'

'I'm there for you any time you want me, Heather,' he said simply, kissing her gently on the mouth and wrapping his arms around her so that the lump swelled in her throat and her eyes blurred with a faint sheen of tears. 'Hey, what's all this?' he murmured, tipping up her chin with his thumb and forefinger. 'I wanted to cheer you up, not make you cry.'

She gave a choked little laugh, and blinked back the tears. 'Then feed me,' she said. 'I'm starving.'

It was a happy meal. Grandad sat with them at the

table in the warm kitchen and tried a little of everything, though he didn't eat much. Ross made them laugh with stories about his student days and later, when Grandad said he was tired, he helped him to his bed.

When Ross came back into the living room he sat down beside her on the settee and put his arm around her shoulders, drawing her close.

'You look all in,' he said softly. 'Go to sleep on me, if you like. I'll check on Sam for you.'

She couldn't sleep, though, not curled up against him this way—so conscious of his nearness, of his arms around her. She lifted her face to his, drinking in his features, and he kissed her, tenderly at first and then with growing passion until they slid down on the soft cushions.

His hands caressed her, shaping her body and exploring the loose edges of her blouse until his palm came to rest possessively on the ripe curve of her breast. Her breath caught as he traced the hardening peak with his thumb, driving her out of her mind with aching need.

She moaned softly and arched her body against his, and he responded instantly, his hand shaking a little as he released the fastening of her bra. He bent his head and slowly claimed the soft flesh of her breast with his mouth, his breath rasping in his throat. The moist, tender touch made her feverish with desire, and when his thigh pressured hers she felt an answering heat and need in him.

'Ah, Heather,' he muttered huskily, 'you're so lovely, so soft and feminine and good to hold.' She clung to him, swirling in a vortex of intense primal desire that was sucking away every shred of her resistance. 'I need you,' he said thickly, trailing kisses over her creamy skin.

Then the clock chimed the hour, and she stilled in

shock, her eyes widening as the sensual moment dissolved and she remembered where they were. 'Ross, I... Ross, we can't...' Her voice was anguished. 'What if my grandad needs me?'

He groaned, lifting his head to gaze down at her face.

'I didn't mean for that to happen,' he muttered, his voice roughened and unsteady. 'I should have had more self-control—but when I'm with you it somehow gets driven away, dissolves in a mist.'

He eased himself away from her. She blinked to clear the fog from her mind, and struggled to restore her clothes to some kind of order.

'I should go and check on him,' she said softly, starting to get up, but his hand gently pushed her down.

'I'll do it. You should get some rest. I'll make sure he's all right. I'll stay—you try to get some sleep.'

He left the room, and Heather leaned back against the cushions and closed her eyes. She had done the right thing, hadn't she, calling a halt? There were all sorts of reasons she ought to keep Ross at bay...but she was just too tired to think of them...

She must have fallen asleep because when she opened her eyes there was daylight seeping into the room, and she realised with a faint sense of shock that she was in her own bed. Her blouse and skirt were folded neatly on a chair, and she had no idea how they had come to be there. Had Ross removed them? He must have. Her cheeks flushed with sudden heat. She was still wearing her bra and briefs, thank heaven—

The front doorbell rang, and she pushed back the duvet with a shaking hand, reaching for her robe. What time was it? Who could that be? And what about Grandad?

Anxiously she hurried out on to the landing, tying the sash of her robe, and met Ross coming out of Grandad's room. Her senses jerked into life at the unexpected sight of him. He must have stayed the whole night while she had slept through. He was alert and full of vigour, and just looking at him made her feel warm inside.

He smiled at her. 'So you're awake. You look better for the rest. It's all right, he's fine,' he said in answer to her unspoken question. 'Take your time. I'll see to the door.'

'Thanks, Ross.'

He gave her a squeeze then went down the stairs, and she put her head round Grandad's door to say hello. He was awake, sitting up in bed, sipping at a cup of tea and glancing through the morning paper.

'What kind of night did you have?' she asked.

'Fair enough,' he said, putting the breakfast tray to one side. There was toast and apricot jam, and Heather realised that she was hungry. 'Ross came and helped me out a couple of times. I'm glad you managed to get some sleep. He's a good man, Heather. You stick by him. You'll do well together.'

Her mouth dropped open for a second or two, then she recovered and said with a smile, 'We do make a good team, don't we? I hadn't expected things to work out so well when I went to work with him.'

His gaze fixed on hers, and she thought how much he resembled her mother, with his direct, practical ways. 'At work and home,' he said. 'I'll rest easy, knowing he's looking after you.' He leaned back against his pillow, a smile of satisfaction on his lips.

How could she argue with him when he was convinced he was right? With a little laugh and a disbelieving shake of her head she smoothed his bed covers and kissed him lightly on his lined forehead.

'You old softy,' she murmured fondly. 'I'll go and

find some breakfast, and then I'll come back and see if there's anything you need help with.'

She went downstairs to the kitchen, still smiling to herself, and watched Ross remove a pan from the hob and pile omelette on to a plate.

He glanced her way. 'There you are,' he said. 'Just in time. Come and eat this while it's hot.' He put the plate on the kitchen table, then came and slid his arm around her waist, drawing her towards a chair. 'Sit down and tuck in. It'll set you up for the day.'

She sat and lifted her face to him. 'Mmm. Smells good. I'm hungry.'

He grinned and dropped a kiss on her soft mouth. 'So am I.'

She didn't think he was talking about food but he moved away from her and went back to the worktop to feed bread into the toaster, and she wondered if she might have imagined that moment of closeness. Pulling her thoughts together, she reached for her fork and said, 'Who was at the door?'

He turned to look at her, then waved a hand towards the sitting-room door behind her.

'Your friend, Martyn. He went to use the phone in the other room. Had to confirm an appointment, I think.'

Shocked, she turned in the direction he'd indicated and saw Martyn, standing in the doorway. His mouth was set in a straight, thin line, and she wondered how long he had been standing there and whether he had witnessed that kiss.

'Martyn,' she gasped in surprise. 'What are you doing here? I wasn't expecting you.'

'I can see that,' he said stiffly, his green eyes raking her slender figure with cool contempt.

Ross lifted out the toast and slid it into the toast rack.

'I had to be in the area for a business meeting this

evening,' Martyn added tersely, 'and I thought it would be a good opportunity to stop by and spend some time with you. Obviously, I thought you would be pleased to see me. I had no idea that you would be...' his gaze lanced towards Ross '...involved.'

Ross's brows lifted briefly and he gave a kind of shrug. Heather had a strong suspicion that he was pleased Martyn thought something was going on.

Ross was busy, setting out another plate on the table. He glanced at Martyn and said amicably, 'Why don't you have a seat, Martyn, and join us for breakfast? I'm just going to take some omelette up to Sam, but don't wait for me. I shall have to rush off and take morning surgery. Help yourself before it gets cold.' He put an arm around Heather's shoulders. 'You too, Heather.'

Ignoring Martyn's scowl, he left the room, and Heather stared after him. He wasn't doing a thing wrong and she owed him for helping her out last night, but none of that did anything to put a lid on her rising temper.

Martyn flicked his glance over Heather, and she flinched under his cold scrutiny and drew the edges of her robe closer together.

'It's not what you think. You're jumping to conclusions,' she told him pointedly.

'Am I?' His nose lifted a fraction and he seemed to grow taller, stiffer, his shoulders going back a notch. Sunlight gleamed on his fair hair. 'So, are you saying that that man didn't spend the night with you?'

'Well, yes, he did stay here,' Heather began, 'but—'

'I don't really think it's necessary for you to say any more, do you, Heather? It's plain to see what's been going on, and why you've found plenty of excuses to stay on here rather than come back home to me. It's not hard to see why you don't want to plan our future together.'

'They aren't excuses,' Heather denied vehemently. 'You're being unfair, disbelieving every word I say. And you could be a little less selfish and try to understand the problems I've been having.'

'Oh, I think I understand them well enough,' Martyn said curtly, glowering at her. 'I believe the main one comes down to a frank choice. Him—or me. What chance do I have as long as you stay on here? I want you to come home, Heather, today—now.'

'I can't do that,' she said quietly, 'and I've already told you that I'm not sure we have a future together.'

'Be reasonable, Heather. I want you to start thinking seriously about what you're leaving behind. What's happened these last months has just been a small glitch in our relationship. We can overcome it. You're under stress, I know, and not able to see things in the proper light, but we've always got along well together. We could have a good life, with the chance to succeed professionally, a decent home and a good standard of living. You can't throw all that away on the strength of a fling with a man you've only just met.'

She studied his features thoughtfully for a while, without saying anything. It was easy enough to appreciate his feelings, but she wasn't about to be pressured into doing anything.

'I think we should get something straight right now,' she said shortly. 'Ross is a friend, someone who's been there for both me and Sam. I'm not living with him, nor have I been sleeping with him, and you have no right to come here and throw accusations about.

'As to the rest, I don't know what I want. You were the one who had it all worked out, but all I know is that I'm mixed up. I have to come to terms with myself and what I want from life before I can include someone else in it.

'I'm happy that you and I are friends, Martyn, but I can't promise anything more than that and I'm not going to be coerced into making decisions about anything until I'm ready. I'm up to here…' she angled her palm against the bridge of her nose '…with men who think they can run my life for me. I shall stay here and look after Grandad for as long as he needs me, and if that's a problem for you then I'm sorry but it's too bad.'

Martyn looked taken aback by her outburst, and she almost felt sorry for him.

'This isn't turning out at all the way I intended,' he said slowly. 'I thought…I'd hoped we could have a few hours together. Go out somewhere, perhaps, before I have to go to this meeting.'

She let out a slow breath. 'We could, I suppose. It depends on whether you're including Grandad in your plans. We were going to spend the day together, and I'm not going to let him down.'

Martyn swallowed. 'If that's what you want…'

'It is.' She pushed her plate away. 'Why don't you go and read the paper or something? I'm going to take a shower now and then I'll help Grandad get ready for the day.'

She met Ross on the stairs.

'I'm off to take surgery,' he said. 'Have you and Martyn sorted out your differences?'

She wasn't fooled by his bland expression of innocence.

'No, thanks to you,' she said tersely. 'You deliberately let him think that something was going on between us. You knew what conclusion he would draw.'

'Was it so far from the truth?' he demanded, raking her flushed features with a searing glance. 'Be honest with yourself, Heather. You weren't thinking about

Martyn last night when you were wrapped in my arms. Far from it. You were with me all the way.'

She gasped, her face blanching. 'That was cruel, it wasn't fair. I was tired and overwrought, I wasn't thinking clearly—'

'Excuses,' he said, with laconic dismissal. 'Face up to reality, Heather. You want me every bit as much as I want you, but you're too much of a coward to admit it, even to yourself.'

He took the rest of the stairs at a brisk pace and went out of the front door, slamming it shut behind him.

Heather stared after him, pressing her fingertips painfully into her palms.

It wasn't true what he'd said, was it? It couldn't be true. She'd been upset, overtired and vulnerable, and that was the only reason she had turned to him. She had come here to escape from having to make any commitment so why did she find herself falling headlong into a situation she couldn't handle?

CHAPTER NINE

As SOON as she had showered and dressed, Heather helped Grandad downstairs and took him into the sitting room to meet Martyn.

'We thought we might all go out this morning,' she said, when she had satisfied herself that Grandad was up to it. 'Where do you fancy going?'

They spent the day in a picturesque little village a few miles away, and found a comfortable place by an old oak where Grandad could sit a while in the shade. They watched the antics of local children, dipping their nets into the brook in search of fish, and when one little girl lost her net and began to shout, Heather went to help. She retrieved it, clambering precariously over large stones in the water, and missed her footing. The little girl clamped a hand to her mouth in dismay as Heather squelched in the water.

'It's all right,' Heather told her. 'It's only my feet, and your net's safe.'

'I don't know why you had to go and do that,' Martyn complained, when she went back to where he was standing. 'Now look at you—you're soaked.'

Heather laughed. 'It doesn't matter—my shoes are only canvas slip-ons, and I'll dry out soon enough in the sunshine. It was fun. It reminded me of the times James and I used to come here with our jam-jars.'

Grandad eyes twinkled. 'And your nan and I would come and wade in with you. They were good days.'

Martyn wasn't appeased. Heather could tell that he was still brooding over the morning, and the atmosphere between them was spoiled from the start. She sighed inwardly and tried to make the best of things.

He drove them home later, and went off to his business meeting. She wouldn't be seeing him again for some time as he was heading north to explore opportunities for new outlets after the meeting, and it saddened her that things were still tense between them.

Grandad patted her hand. 'He didn't take to Ross, being on the scene, did he? Never mind, love. Things have a way of sorting themselves out.'

She looked at him thoughtfully. He looked remarkably pleased with himself.

Ross called at the cottage the next day to see Grandad. Heather let him in, unhappily aware of a welter of conflicting emotions at the sight of him. Her first instinct was to put up a defensive barrier between them. She didn't want to be attracted to him in any way, yet every time he was near her she was conscious of this strong, magnetic pull. She had to resist it. Too many things could go wrong if she allowed her feelings free rein where he was concerned. Look at the way things had turned out with Martyn. She simply wasn't good at relationships. She didn't have any faith in their durability and, if she was honest with herself, she was afraid of getting hurt.

'I don't see your boyfriend around,' Ross remarked coolly, breaking into her thoughts, and she wondered if he had the uncanny knack of reading her mind.

'Martyn had to go back to work—the next leg of my father's expansion programme.' She led the way along the hall.

His eyes narrowed on her. 'That must be difficult for you.'

She thought she detected a cynical note in his voice,

and she stiffened, returning his glance with a measure of frost.

'I expect I shall cope, very much as I have done before.'

'How very cool and practical.' His dark eyes mocked her. 'What's wrong? Doesn't he turn you on?'

'That's none of your business!' she hissed angrily. 'We just work together, you and I. Let's keep it that way, shall we?'

'A professional distance between us—is that what you're saying?'

She breathed in deeply. 'That's exactly what I'm saying.'

He gave a harsh laugh. 'You weren't so cold and remote the other evening. Just the opposite, in fact.' His eyes glittered devilishly and she glared at him.

'I don't want to think about that, or talk about it,' she said unevenly. 'Just forget it ever happened, will you?'

His mouth twisted. 'I'll do my best.' He came to a halt at the door to the living room. 'Is Sam in here?'

'Yes. He didn't have too bad a night, but he's weary.' Her voice dropped. 'I'm getting concerned about him. I'd hoped he might show some signs of improvement, but it isn't happening.'

He grimaced. 'Then maybe we should declare a truce and make the most of what's left of the summer, for his sake,' he suggested. 'We could take him out and about. He loves the countryside, and there might not be too many chances left.'

Heather couldn't help but agree. They both knew that his condition was worsening, and she wanted to do whatever she could to make him happy.

It was settled, and they arranged several outings. Toby went with them, and they worked together to ensure that the days were full of laughter and contentment. They enjoyed the fresh air, and the smell of grass, and listened to the sound of water, burbling over rocks.

James came for a visit on the day before the summer bank holiday. He had brought pictures with him that the children had drawn for Grandad, and Heather felt a dampness in her eyes as she watched Sam's face light up with pleasure.

'They'd have come with me, but they've both gone down with chickenpox,' he said.

'Poor mites,' Grandad murmured. 'They'll miss our day out.'

'Are you feeling well enough to take a trip out today?' Ross asked him. He had been looking more tired than usual, Heather thought, and she'd had her own doubts that he would want to go.

'Yes, I'd like that,' Grandad said, so they packed a blanket in the car, along with a picnic basket and a lounger for Sam, and the four of them set off.

They sat by a pond and ate the food she'd prepared, then fed crumbs to the ducks.

Ross threw sticks for Toby, and James watched them for a while, then said quietly to Heather, 'Things didn't go too well for you, then, when Martyn came over?'

She made a rueful mouth. 'You heard about that, did you?'

'Martyn said a few things to dad about it.'

'Ouch!' Heather grimaced.

James chuckled. 'That's what I thought, too. Ouch! Let's just say, Dad thinks you're making a big mistake, not to mention being selfish in not supporting his protégé.'

'Perhaps I am.'

Grandad shook his head. 'It's your life, girl. You're the only one who can decide what's best for you. You, too, James. Bear it in mind. Laura's a good woman.

Parents often try to influence their offspring—it goes along with the job—but it comes down to you in the end.'

He stopped, his breathing laboured so that Heather glanced at him, hiding her concern. He settled, though, and she said with a faint frown, 'I wouldn't mind so much if I thought Dad really cared about me. I've never really believed he even liked me very much and the thing is, I've never understood why.'

Ross came and sat beside them, and Grandad said thoughtfully, 'It could be that he thinks you're not his. I'm not saying, mind, that there's any justification in him thinking that,' he added at her startled gasp, 'but that's the impression I always had.'

Heather was stunned, and Ross's arm came around her comfortingly. 'If he thought there was another man then the rest follows,' he murmured, 'but that doesn't mean it's true. You said yourself that your father doesn't see things from any point of view but his own.'

She gave a weak smile. 'You could be right, I suppose.'

'I wouldn't let it worry you,' James put in. 'As Grandad says, it's not likely to be true, but it would account for Dad's behaviour all these years.'

Heather's mouth twisted. 'You know, I actually feel as though a weight's been lifted from me,' she said. 'All these years I wondered, and now it all makes a kind of sense.'

She met Grandad's gaze, and they smiled at each other with understanding.

'You'll be all right, girl,' he said. His eyes closed and he rested his head back against his cushioned seat.

She turned to Ross. 'You get on well with your parents, don't you?'

'Always have done. It's not an easy job, is it? But

they seem to have the balance about right.' His arm was still around her and it felt just right, as though it belonged. She could have stayed like that for ever, sheltered in his embrace.

After some time, though, she noticed that the sun was less warm and Grandad looked tired.

'Is it time we went home, do you think? We could finish off the day in the garden with a barbecue.'

They went along with her suggestion, and a while later Ross and James organised the barbecue, while Heather settled Grandad on the bench in the garden with a blanket around him.

'Are you comfy?' she asked, noting the weary lines in his face, and he nodded, a gentle smile on his mouth.

'I always sat here of an evening with my Jen.' He patted the seat beside him. 'Come and sit with me, lass.'

She sat with him and put her hand on his. 'You and Nan were the best grandparents in the world,' she told him.

His mouth curved. 'I'm glad you three are here with me. Jenny would have enjoyed today.' Still smiling, he closed his eyes, and went into a little doze.

Heather ate some of the food Ross and James prepared, but Grandad was still sleeping and they thought better of disturbing him. They talked quietly for a while, and Heather glanced at Grandad from time to time and put her hand over his once more.

She wasn't sure how long they all sat there, chatting about this and that, but she looked at Grandad again in a while and became conscious of a change in him. Her breath snagged in her lungs, and her gaze shot to Ross.

'I know,' he said softly, and came to sit beside her, his hands curving about her shoulders to give her strength.

'He's so still,' she whispered, 'so peaceful. Oh,

Ross...I think he's gone...' Tears filled her eyes, and she heard James's indrawn breath.

He came to crouch in front of the bench and took Sam's other hand in his, biting his lip to keep his jaw from working. Heather leaned forward and put her arms around him.

'I thought it might happen today,' Ross said huskily. 'I had a feeling...'

Heather saw the bright sheen in his eyes, and knew that he felt the loss every bit as keenly as they did. She turned to hold him and comfort him in return, glad above all that he was here right now. She desperately needed him to be with her.

The next few days passed in a blur of sorrow and tears, and Heather knew she couldn't have gone through any of it without Ross by her side. James stayed on, keeping her company in the cottage, and she felt guilty for wishing it had been Ross who had stayed each night. He was never far away, though.

He helped her to deal with all the arrangements for the funeral, and he stood beside her and James at the graveside on that cool, damp day when Grandad was finally laid to rest.

'I miss him,' she whispered.

'So do I,' Ross said. 'He was a good age, though, and he had a good life.' He was trying to comfort her, even though he was going through much the same grief. 'He was convinced that death wasn't the end and that he would meet up again with his Jenny.'

'I know,' Heather said, wiping away the trickle of salty tears from her cheeks. 'Who knows? He may be right.'

They made the journey back to the cottage, and she talked to Frank and Harry and his other friends who had come to pay their respects, and she tried to keep a hold on her emotions. She served sandwiches and tea, and somehow managed to get through it all.

James was there with Laura, but they weren't talking much, and Heather wondered how he was coping, how much of his tension was there because of the funeral and how much was a result of the strained atmosphere between him and his wife as they both tried to put their differences to one side.

Laura spoke to her briefly but she was as stressed as James, her features tight, as though she was holding herself in check.

After an hour or so Ross came and murmured quietly, 'I have to go and check on Toby.'

She understood, but that didn't stop the rush of loneliness that swamped her as he left the house. She stiffened her shoulders and turned her attention back to her guests.

She managed to get James alone for a few minutes as he was preparing to leave. 'How are things between you and Laura?' she asked quietly.

'About as bad as they can be,' he admitted. 'I don't know how much longer we can stay together. I don't want to lose the children—but we can't go on the way we are, with all the arguments. It's affecting the children—and my nerves are shot to pieces. My stomach's on fire, my concentration's gone. I feel as though I'm strung out like a tennis racket.'

She touched his arm in sympathy. 'At least she's come with you today. Isn't that a good sign?'

'She wanted to be here for Grandad. If it hadn't been for the arguments between us, she'd have come to see him before.'

'I'm so sorry.' He looked thoroughly miserable and she wished there was something she could do to help.

'Is there any chance things could get better? If there's anything worth saving in your marriage, surely you should put up a fight? You're feeling low now, but this is a bad day and you've been overworking for such a long time. You need a rest as much as anything.'

He had to say goodbye soon after that, and she didn't envy him the long drive home. After he had gone she kept up a show of being in command of herself as the people who had crowded into the cottage began to take their leave, but she felt unreal, as though it wasn't her, talking and moving among them. Then Ross came back, bringing Toby with him, and her spirits lifted a little.

She felt drained after everyone had left. At least Ross was here, though, and she knew that he sensed her need of him, and that she didn't want to stay alone in the cottage where her grandad's presence was still so acutely felt.

She turned to him as quiet descended on the house, and he gathered her into his arms and pressed his lips to her hair in a gentle caress.

'You've been my rock,' she muttered huskily, 'my strength. I don't know how I would have managed without you. I feel empty inside, as though I'm living in a vacuum, doing what I have to just to get through the days.'

'We're here for each other,' he said. He touched her cheek with his and added, 'You're cold. Come and sit with me by the fire, and I'll warm you.'

He drew her over to the settee and tugged her down beside him, putting an arm around her so that she could snuggle against him, resting her cheek against his chest. His fingers gently stroked her hair, soothing her until some of the tension in her eased and her breathing slowed and became more restful. She felt the steady rhythm of his heartbeat, and it gradually calmed her, making her eyelids seem heavy.

'Will you stay?' she mumbled into his shirt.

'Of course I will. I planned to once James had gone home. That's why I brought Toby with me. I can imagine how vulnerable you must be feeling just now. It isn't just Sam you're grieving for, but your mother and your Nan… Times like these bring it all back.'

He understood what she was going through, without her having to say anything at all, and she hugged him tight, thankful for his calm, soothing presence.

He stayed with her that night, comforting her and holding her close whenever she needed him—his tender kisses melting away the edges of that cold place in her heart. She sensed the restraint in him, the careful control he exercised when it would have been so easy for their nearness to turn into passion.

She put her hand to his face, cupping his cheek. Tired though she was, she recognised that it wasn't enough to be held like this. Deep down she wanted more, and she lifted her gaze to him.

'Thanks for being here, Ross…when I needed you most…'

'I wanted to be here with you,' he murmured. 'I want you, Heather…' He put a finger to her lips as she opened her mouth to mumble incoherent, confused words, and he added softly, 'But this isn't the right time. You're still hung over with the events of the last few days, and your mind isn't clear. I want you to be very clear about what's happening between us, Heather. I want you to be very sure about what you're doing, and at this moment I think you're too weary and too overshadowed with grief to be sure of anything.'

She had to accept that he was probably right. These last few months she had been confused about so many things, her emotions veering from extreme to the other. He always had the balance about right…she could trust his judgement…she was simply too tired to think straight just now…

When she woke in the morning her first instinct was to reach for him—but when her fingers touched the cold pillow she remembered that he had stayed downstairs to lock up and see to the fire and the hearth, and that he was going to sleep in the spare bedroom.

Slowly, her thoughts came around to the day. She would make breakfast, then ask him about his plans for the weekend.

The phone rang as she was fetching juice from the fridge, and she went to answer it, warming to Ross's circling embrace as she brushed by him. She flattened her palm against his chest, though, resisting him as she caught the smell of over-crisped bacon and reached to turn off the gas. The phone was still ringing, distracting her thoughts, and she lifted the receiver to shut off the noise.

'Martyn…'

'Heather, darling.' His voice was huskily apologetic. 'I'm sorry I couldn't be with you these last few days. It must have been dreadful for you, having to cope.'

'I managed,' she said.

'Of course you did. You always manage everything beautifully. Look, I must see you soon. There's so much we have to say to each other, things we need to talk over properly.'

She bit her lip, and said quietly, 'Yes, you're right. We should meet. It's just that I don't know when I can get away…there's so much to sort out.' Her mind clouded over. She had known how ill Grandad was, but she still hadn't been prepared.

'I can imagine. There'll be all kinds of things to arrange. You'll need to sell the cottage, of course.'

'Sell the cottage?' she echoed, and then the reality of the situation began to dawn on her and the chill of loneliness crept into her heart. Her life here with Grandad had truly come to an end. She didn't belong here any more.

'Heather?' Martyn prompted, and she swallowed hard and tried to get herself together. She wasn't ready for this. She was still grieving, her mind was shutting down, refusing to take anything in.

'I suppose you're right. I'll have to. I hadn't thought that far ahead.'

'You don't have to deal with this alone,' he said. 'I'm on my way to you now. I just stopped off at a service station.'

She made an effort to take in what he was saying. 'I hadn't realised you'd already started out. How long will it be before you get here?'

'About half an hour or so. Let me check the map. I've come by a different route today.'

Beside her she felt Ross stiffen, and she turned to look up at him.

'He's coming here?' he asked.

She nodded, frowning. 'He wants to talk. I think we should. There's a lot we have to sort out.'

His expression froze, and then slowly he turned and walked to the door.

She watched him and said quickly, 'You're not going, are you?'

'I promised my parents I'd go and visit them,' he murmured, pausing as he pulled the door open. 'Since you're going to be with Martyn, I may as well go now. I'll see you back at the surgery on Monday.'

'But—' Just as she was calling after him, Martyn's

voice came back on the line, demanding her attention. She cut the call and hurried after Ross, but she was too late. His car door slammed, and his engine revved as he drove away, leaving a cloud of exhaust fumes and a cold, lonely place in her chest.

Why had he gone? She desperately wished that he had stayed. In her darkest hour she had turned blindly to Ross, and now she felt lost without him. She felt like crying all over again, but Martyn was on his way and she had to pull herself together somehow to say what she had to say.

Martyn hadn't been there for her when she needed a friend, and it occurred to her that it had never crossed her mind to seek him out. They weren't compatible at all, she realised. He had never been able to understand her love for her grandfather, and her need to be with him, and even now his thoughts were only centred on practical things.

She knew now that she had to finish things between them once and for all, and this time she would make sure that he accepted it. He would be here soon, and the least she could do was tell him face to face.

He arrived within the hour, and she told him what she had decided as gently as she could. He took it badly, but she had made up her mind and it was only fair to make him see that she wasn't going to back down.

'It's Ross Kennedy, isn't it? He's the one who got in the way.'

'He didn't get in the way,' she told him quietly. 'He just helped me to see things more clearly. I came to realise that I can't marry you because I would never be able to give you the love you deserve. I couldn't make you happy, Martyn. I look around me and I see marriages falling apart all the time, and I don't want to add to their number. It wouldn't be fair to commit us both to a relationship that had no chance from the start.'

'I'm willing enough to give it a try,' he said gruffly.

'I'm not,' she said simply. 'I'm sorry, Martyn, but I've made my decision. It's over.'

On Monday morning Heather went back to work and immersed herself in routine. Ross came into Reception to check his post, before going out on his calls, but—apart from a brief greeting—there was no familiar warmth of contact between them. He was remote, distancing himself from her behind a wall of work, and that made her hesitate and pull back from approaching him. She didn't understand what had happened. Had he decided that their last evening together had been a mistake? There had been the funeral that day, and they had both been vulnerable, needing each other.

Feeling sad and lonely, she went through to her room and shut herself away, ringing the bell for her first patient.

She worked steadily until it was nearly lunchtime, then saw that Louise was her last patient of the morning. She didn't look well, and Heather felt a rush of concern that she did her best to damp down.

'You've gained more weight than I'd have expected,' she murmured, checking the scales. 'From the puffiness of your ankles and hands, it could be due to water retention. Let's check your blood pressure before we go any further.'

'It's probably high again,' Louise said with a slight grimace. 'It's this place that does it, you know. Full of sick people and problems to be solved.' She gave a mock shudder, and Heather smiled faintly.

'A lot of people feel that way. Still, your blood pressure is definitely higher than it should be, and I'm not happy about your urine sample. There's some protein in it, and it all adds up to the fact that you need supervised rest. In hospital, I'm afraid.'

Louise shook her head. 'I knew you would say that. I can't possibly go to hospital. It's out of the question.'

Heather looked her straight in the eyes and said quietly, 'You do want the best for this baby, don't you?'

'Well, of course I do. But it isn't that serious, is it?'

'Yes, it is, I'm afraid. You must know it too, deep down, Louise. For your baby's sake, and your own, you must go to hospital for a while until we get your blood pressure down and everything as it should be.'

'I can't,' Louise said again. 'John's away at an important conference, and there's Ben to think of. There's no one to take care of him.'

'Where is he now?'

'With a neighbour. But she has to go out later.'

'I'm sure Ross and I can work something out,' Heather said firmly. 'I expect he'll be back from his calls any time now. We'll talk to him about it.'

Ross arrived a few minutes later, and Heather noticed the stiff line of his shoulders, the brisk, no-nonsense air of a man who was concentrating determinedly on getting the job done.

Quickly she outlined the problem, hoping that he would be supportive because Louise was in an emotional state. 'Between us, we could look after him, couldn't we?' she said. 'He liked the garden at the cottage—he can come over and play on the swing and kick a ball about when you're busy with other things.'

To her relief, he nodded. 'No problem. He can stay with me. We'll sort something out.' He squeezed Louise's hand affectionately. 'With both of us taking care of him, and playschool in between, you've nothing to worry about. Come on, sis, let's get you organised and into hospital.'

They talked to the neighbour and managed to work out a plan of action that satisfied Louise. Once the arrangements had been taken care of, they helped her to pack a few things and supervised her move to the maternity unit. She was feeling low and a bit tearful, and they both hugged her, promising to bring Ben at visiting time. They left her talking to John on the phone.

Heather walked back to the car with Ross, aware that his stiff, unapproachable manner had returned as soon as they'd left the ward. It was the wrong time to try to talk to him, she sensed. Whatever she said, she would finish up having her head snapped off.

She suppressed a sigh and climbed into his car. They had just started for home when Ross's phone bleeped and Heather picked it up to take the call.

'Manor Farm,' she told him after a minute. 'Richard Stanway's had a fall, a possible leg injury. The farm's on our way, isn't it? We may as well go together.'

'OK.' He turned the car in the direction of the farm, and they arrived there within a matter of minutes.

Richard was out in a barn where he had been checking the animal feed and had fallen from a ladder. He was in a good deal of pain, and Heather knelt down beside him to assess the damage.

'Damn fool thing to do. I missed a step and lost my hold on the thing,' he said through clenched teeth.

'It's your knee that's the biggest problem, I think, Richard,' she said, gently probing the swollen joint. 'Possibly the fall has inflamed the tissues that were already damaged because of your condition. We won't really know without an X-ray. I expect it will mean a couple of days in hospital for observation because your spine took a bit of a knock as well. Don't worry, we'll make you as comfortable as we can.'

Ross organised his transfer to hospital, while Heather took the opportunity to talk to the farmer and try to glean what information she could about Richard's family.

'He hasn't seen anything of them since he's been down here,' the farmer said, scratching his head, 'but I think I might have a phone number on his employment form. I could look it up for you, if you like.'

'Thanks.' Heather followed him into the farmhouse to gather the details, then went back to the car to use the mobile phone.

Ross came to join her as she was talking to Richard's mother.

'That's right,' she was saying to the anxious woman. 'He's on his way there now.'

She cut the call and glanced up at Ross.

'What was that about?' he asked with a frown.

'I spoke to Richard's mother,' she told him flatly.

His mouth tightened. 'Richard didn't want his parents to know—it isn't our place to countermand his decisions. You shouldn't have done that, Heather.'

Heather shrugged. 'It was my decision to make the call and I stand by it,' she said coolly. 'I'm quite prepared to deal with the consequences of my actions—you don't have to be involved in any way.'

'Of course I'm involved,' he said tautly. 'I'm the head of the practice, I'm supposed to be kept fully informed of any decisions regarding our patients and I expect you to abide by the ones we've made together. You were well aware of my feelings on this score and you deliberately went against what we had agreed.'

She was taken aback by his vehemence, but she stood her ground. 'As I see it, Richard wanted his parents kept in the dark about his illness. Nothing was ever said about accidents, and I did what I felt was necessary. I stand by that decision,' she said firmly. 'If he were my son, I'd want to know if he was being sent to hospital. I would hope someone would think to tell me. If you're not happy with that then I'm sorry, but it changes nothing. I'd do the same again.'

'And I'm just supposed to accept it?' he rasped. 'No discussion, no mutual decision-making?'

Heather's jaw clenched. 'You're not around every minute of my working day. There are some things I have to decide on my own.'

'And others can wait until we've had a chance to talk them through,' he shot back. 'That's how the system works.'

Her fingers tightened. 'Arguing like this is getting us nowhere,' she said. 'Perhaps it's just as well that my contract with you finishes in a few weeks' time. It will give you the chance to find someone more agreeable to work with.'

He switched on the ignition and gunned the accelerator. 'You're right,' he said crisply. 'It certainly will. I'll organise an advert for your replacement. With any luck, it will go out this week.'

The journey back to the practice was a silent one, both of them occupied with their own thoughts. Heather was miserably aware that even though the words had been spoken in anger they were basically the truth. What reason was there for her to stay here, after all, now that Grandad had gone? She had the Malvern job to consider, and the time for her to make her decision was drawing near.

Perhaps if Ross had felt differently about things... But he had just made it very clear that he didn't want her around, and how could she work with him, anyway, if he was going to be as overbearing as he had been this afternoon? All her life she had battled with her father in a similar vein, and she didn't want to go the same way with Ross. Deep down, perhaps, she had hoped he might be different.

Ross glanced at his watch. 'It's time to collect Ben,' he said briefly. 'Shall I drop you off at the surgery or at the cottage?'

She was surprised that he was giving her a choice. 'I'd assumed I was going along with you. You'll need help to sort out Ben's overnight things, and there'll be his toys to collect.'

'I'm sure I can manage my own nephew, without having to lean on you.' His tone was abrupt and she flinched, stung by the rejection.

'But Louise told him we would both be taking care of him,' Heather pointed out. 'For Ben's sake, I think we should work together on this, without letting our feelings get in the way. Don't you agree? It's not going to help him adjust to the fact that his mother's in hospital if we start changing the arrangements now, nor will it help if we are at loggerheads all the time.'

'As you please,' he said shortly, and swung the car in the direction of Louise's neighbour's house, leaving Heather miserably aware of just how much things had deteriorated between them.

It hurt, but she had to push it to the back of her mind and put on a bright face for Ben.

'I could take him over to the cottage for an hour or so before late surgery, if it will help,' she suggested.

'I don't think so.' His tone was curt as he pulled up outside the neighbour's house. 'He might want to know where Sam is, and I'd rather not give him any more unfortunate happenings to dwell on.'

She hadn't thought of that. He was probably right, but it felt like a rebuff, and she subsided into silence, aware that whatever she said right now was likely to be the wrong thing. All she could do was try to weather the storm, and she braced her shoulders and followed him to the house.

'Is my daddy coming home?' Ben asked, and Heather wondered how it must be to have his world disrupted like this.

'Tomorrow, sweetheart. You'll be staying with Uncle Ross until then so we'll need to fetch some of your things from home. We'll go and get them now, shall we?'

Ben slid his small hand into Ross's, and they all went to gather up some of his belongings. Heather watched the two of them and listened to their chat as they decided on which things to take and which to leave. It brought a lump to her throat to see them together and to recognise the bond of affection that existed between them.

'Will you come with us to Uncle Ross's house?' Ben asked, and her glance flew to Ross. His eyes were dark and unfathomable, not giving anything away, and Heather wasn't sure what to say. She didn't want Ben to be upset in any way, but Ross's hostility, veiled or otherwise, was hard to take.

'I do have to go to the surgery,' she compromised, 'but I'll be close by.'

'Good,' Ben said, his eyes sparkling. 'You can read me a story. Mummy always reads me a story at bedtime.'

Ross turned away and picked up the assortment of clothing and toys they had assembled, and then said laconically, 'Let's go.'

Heather found her own hand being tugged by the little one this time, and they headed back to the car. Children were sensitive to atmosphere, and both she and Ross were doing their best not to let him see their coolness towards each other but it wasn't easy. It seemed to take a lot of effort to keep up a happy façade when inside she was breaking up. Was this how alienated parents felt, when dealing with their offspring?

Ben seemed blissfully unaware, though, and from the looks of things he had settled in happily enough at Ross's house. He extracted a promise from Heather that she would go back and play with him after surgery was finished.

It was an uneventful surgery and she finished her list in good time so that she went back into Ross's living room to find the two of them playing on the rug with a toy farm.

Ben was in his pyjamas, his face clean and his hair neatly brushed. He was moving the cows about the field, and both he and Ross were making mooing sounds. Heather watched them quietly for a minute, her mouth curving.

Then Ross looked up, still smiling, and Ben patted the carpet beside him. 'Come and play with us.'

Heather got down on the mat with them and joined in. She herded cows and shepherded sheep for a while until Ben yawned and Ross looked at the clock.

'Time for the animals to go into the barn to sleep,' he said to the boy, and after a minute or two they tidied the game away.

Ben went into the bathroom to clean his teeth, and Heather picked out a storybook from the pile on the coffee-table while Ross cleared away the supper things.

'You were having fun,' she said softly, her glance meshing with his. 'You're very good with him. I can imagine you with a family of your own.'

He paused, and his smile faded. 'For that to happen, the right woman would need to come along. Perhaps one day.'

Heather's fingers tightened on the book. She had said

it unthinkingly, and now she thought about the woman who might one day bear Ross's children and something twisted painfully in her chest.

She went upstairs, tucked Ben into bed and sat with him, reading quietly until his eyelids started to droop. The light in the room was dimmed, and she carefully put the book to one side and bent to kiss the sleepy child. Then she turned towards the door and saw Ross standing there, his features shadowed, his eyes shuttered. She didn't know how long he had been there.

'I came to say goodnight to him,' he murmured, and walked over to the bed, smoothing the bed covers and dropping a light kiss on Ben's forehead.

Heather went out onto the landing and started down the stairs. She heard Ross quietly close the bedroom door and come after her, and she went to the living room to get her jacket.

'Will you stay a while?' he asked, and she might have been sorely tempted except that his tone was faintly abrupt and she couldn't be sure that he wasn't asking her out of mere politeness. That would be more than she could stand right now. If she was honest with herself, what she really wanted was for him to put his arms around her and hold her close, and that wasn't likely to happen, was it? He was still looking for the woman who would be his soulmate, and the irony of it was that just when it was probably too late she was beginning to wish it might be her.

That wasn't possible, though, she realised with a growing feeling of emptiness inside, not when he had made it plain he was looking for her successor at the practice.

'I don't think so,' she said quietly. 'I have some things I need to do back at the cottage. Some clearing up. I've been putting off going through Grandad's things, but I should get on with it and put the house in order.'

'Ready to sell?'

'I suppose so. I'll talk it through with the solicitor some time in the next week or so.'

His expression was unreadable, and she turned and went to the door, too choked to say any more just now. She needed desperately to get away from him before she broke down completely.

CHAPTER TEN

THE next few weeks were harder to cope with than Heather could have ever imagined. Perhaps it was the aftermath of Grandad passing away, but she found the widening gulf between herself and Ross unbearably difficult to take. Whenever she saw him there was this aching void inside her, and more often than not she felt close to tears.

It wouldn't do, of course, and the only way she could deal with the situation was to bury herself in her work and hope that dealing with other people's problems would take the edge off some of her own.

Louise came out of hospital, looking much better for the rest and determined not to have to go back in until her contractions started and labour was imminent.

A few days later Natalie Fraser came into the surgery and asked for a pregnancy test. Heather confirmed that the result was positive, and Natalie managed to look pleased and anxious at the same time.

'We wouldn't have planned to have a baby yet under normal circumstances,' she explained, 'but, with things going wrong last time, I want to know that I can have one properly. I couldn't wait years, not knowing.'

Heather could understand her reasoning, even as she wondered what kind of life the child would have. It would be loved, though, she felt sure, seeing Natalie's gentle smile.

'I'll organise a scan for you,' she told her. 'That should tell us if things are proceeding as they should.' She wrote out the form and handed it to Natalie. 'Take that to Reception and they'll fix up an appointment at the hospital.'

Surgery was a long one that day, with tricky paediatric problems and a crop of ear, nose and throat infections that made Heather glad she had a strong constitution.

After she had worked her way to the end of her list she was tidying her desk when the receptionist asked if she was free to fit in one more appointment.

Heather agreed and looked up to see a thin, dark-haired woman, whose forehead bore deep worry lines. With her was a taller man, straight-backed, his features austere, as though he was holding himself in check.

She glanced at the appointment card. 'Mr and Mrs Stanway...What can I do for you?'

'We've been to see Richard in hospital,' the woman said, sitting down. Mr Stanway looked uncomfortable but remained standing, even though Heather motioned him to a chair. 'His knee was damaged as a result of the fall,' Mrs Stanway went on, 'but the doctor told us his underlying condition had made him more susceptible.'

Heather wondered just how much they had been told, or whether they had enquired into the situation at all, but she waited to see what they volunteered, asking simply, 'How is he? I haven't received the report from the hospital yet.'

'He came out last week,' Mrs Stanway answered. 'He has to take things easy for a while They say he might need an operation to replace the joint some time in the future, but for now they're going to treat him with tablets and physiotherapy. We had no idea what he had been going through. He kept it to himself—I suppose he didn't think it was macho to complain. He wanted to be like his friends, but he couldn't keep up.'

'If he'd just said something—anything—' Richard's

father put in, then broke off, his jaw working spasmodically.

His wife glanced at him, then said carefully, 'I always wondered if something was wrong—but when he was younger it was always put down to growing pains.'

Mr Stanway gripped the back of his wife's chair, his knuckles whitening under the pressure. 'If I'd known... I thought he needed building up, that plenty of sport would be the thing, but, of course, he wasn't strong enough for that—it just made matters worse.'

Heather shook her head. 'I doubt that you did anything to worsen his condition, but you're probably right in that strenuous physical activity would have been beyond him at that time.' She looked from one to the other. 'Have you spoken to the consultant about his illness?'

'Yes.' Mrs Stanway nodded. 'He explained it all to us. That's why we're here, really. We wanted to thank you for letting us know what was happening.'

'If it had been left to Richard, we'd still be in the dark,' Mr Stanway said flatly.

'How does Richard feel about things now?' Heather asked. She'd acted with his interests in mind, and she hoped he wasn't resenting the fact that his parents had become involved.

'I think he's relieved we've had a chance to talk things through.' For the first time Mr Stanway's features relaxed. 'We can't persuade him to come home because he has his job at the farm to think of, and he's made new friends there, but at least now we'll keep in regular contact with him.'

'I'm glad about that,' Heather said with a smile, 'and I'm glad you spared the time to come along to give me the news.'

She saw them out, and went along to Reception to

deal with her paperwork. Ross was there, signing repeat prescriptions, and he sent her a querying look.

'What did the Stanways want?'

Heather's shoulders went back and she braced herself for more trouble. His mood hadn't changed much since that day at the farm, but she wasn't going to back down.

'To thank me for letting them know about Richard.'

His eyes darkened. 'We never did talk that through.'

She cut in before he could say any more. 'What would be the point now? I shan't be here for much longer, shall I?' Her fingers sifted restlessly through the papers in her tray. 'What's the news on my replacement? Have you had any replies to your advert?'

'A few.' His gaze meshed coolly with hers. 'I'll have to make a shortlist.'

He wasn't going to have much trouble replacing her, then. It was a depressing thought, that she could just cease to be a part of his life, but she didn't want him to see that it bothered her so she picked a letter from her tray and scanned its contents, hardly aware of a word that was written there.

'How's the business of selling the cottage going along? Have you put a notice up yet?'

She shook her head. That was another thing she didn't want to think about. Selling the house that held such wonderful memories for her would be like losing part of herself. 'I ought to phone James and sort out the arrangements with him. He might want to go along with me to see the solicitor—and I suppose I should pay a visit to an estate agent.'

'Haven't you done anything at all about it yet?'

'Not yet. I imagine there's a Will so maybe that's the first step, finding out what Grandad wanted.'

'You mean you don't know?' His brow lifted in surprise.

'It never came up. Or, if it did, I brushed the subject aside. I didn't want to think about it.'

'He left everything to you and your brother.'

It was her turn to be startled. 'He told you that?'

'He wanted to make sure that you were both provided for. It doesn't necessarily mean you have to sell, though.'

She thought about that, wistfully wondering how it would be if things were different and she could stay on here. Then she repressed a sigh and said, 'But James would find the money useful, I dare say, with his family to bring up and the mortgage round his neck. I really must ring him.'

Ross waved a hand towards the phone. 'No time like the present.'

Heather's stomach muscles twisted. Was he so anxious to be rid of her? All the same, he was probably right—she had been putting it off for long enough.

She dialled James's number and after a minute or two he answered. He sounded harassed.

'Is this a bad time?' she asked. 'I was only ringing to see what you want to do about seeing a solicitor to deal with Grandad's estate. I could always ring back later.'

'I don't mind what you do, Heather. Do you want to deal with it from your end? I'll help you out all I can, but right now I'm up to my ears in it. I've so much to sort out. Laura's threatening to walk out on me, and Dad's insisting I work the weekend and go over some files with him or I have to think again about my position with the firm. I've so many people on my back. To be honest, Heather, I don't think I can take much more.'

'Why don't you take five minutes for yourself, and think about what *you* want for a change?' she suggested quietly. 'Remember what Grandad said? Do what's best for you.'

She put the phone down a few minutes later, still deep in thought, and her hand brushed against Ross's as she turned back to her tray. Her fingers seemed to burn from the contact and she drew her hand back sharply, her glance darting to meet his.

His mouth twisted in a cynical line at her abrupt withdrawal, but he said straightforwardly enough, 'Problems?'

'He's very stressed,' she admitted. 'I think they're on the verge of splitting up.'

He started to say something, but the receptionist came and touched his arm and he went off with her to check a patient's details on the computer.

Heather stacked the papers neatly in her tray and went to get her jacket. She was strangely weary, and the prospect of going back to a lonely supper at the cottage was making her even more unsettled. Still, there was nothing for her here either, she reflected miserably, since Ross was determined to shut her out. At least at home she could lick her wounds in private.

Heather was on call on Friday afternoon, and it was getting towards dusk when she finished her scheduled visits and let herself into the cottage. She had scarcely had time to make herself a sandwich when the phone rang.

'Heather, it's Ross.' He sounded as though he was in a hurry. 'Louise has gone into labour and I need to get her to hospital. John's on his way back, but he won't be here for another hour yet, and Mum and Dad are *en route* from a trip to the coast. Can I ask a favour?'

'Of course. What is it, do you want me to fetch Ben?'

'No, he's with a neighbour. It's Toby I was thinking about. He probably needs to be let out of the house for a run in the garden—and he'll be ready for a meal by now. Would you mind going over there? I'll get back as soon as I can.'

'Don't worry about it. I'll go there now. Give Louise my love.'

'I will.'

He cut the call and left her with only the echoes of his deep, warm voice, vibrating inside her head. She thought about him for a minute, dreamily conjuring up his image, before she pulled herself together and went out to the car. Officially, she was on duty for another couple of hours, and with a bit of luck it would be a quiet evening.

Toby greeted her ecstatically, thumping everything around him with his tail. She fetched his lead and took him for a walk along the lane, then went back to the house and opened the door to the garden to let him out. He dashed in again when he heard the sound of his supper being prepared, and Heather watched him wolf it down with a rueful shake of her head.

'Thirty seconds to demolish the lot! You have absolutely no table manners.'

She went into the living room and glanced through a magazine for a while, her concentration shot as she wondered how Louise was getting on and whether Ross would be back soon. Toby settled down at her feet, his head on his paws, keeping an eye on her as though he was afraid she might slip away from him.

'Were you feeling lonely too?' she murmured, looking down at him and stroking his head. 'I don't see what you have to complain about. You have him to yourself every day.' Then her phone started to ring and startled both of them.

'Dr Brooks? It's Natalie Fraser here.'

Heather's first instinct was that Natalie might be having trouble with this pregnancy, too, and she was immediately alert.

Natalie went on, 'Will you come over to my mum's house? She's very dizzy and her chest hurts badly and I'm afraid she's going to pass out.'

'I'll be with you in a few minutes,' Heather promised, and went to get her medical bag. Was Kevin Fraser likely to be on the scene? Probably. She debated what to do if he was in an aggressive mood, and then Toby whined and rubbed against her leg. She looked down at him. 'Do you want to come with me?' His tail thumped. 'OK. I'd better leave a note for Ross, or he'll wonder where you are.'

She scribbled a note and left it on the table, then went out to her car and let Toby inside. It was getting dark now, and she drove carefully, parking in the road outside the Frasers' house. Toby went to jump out, but she told him to stay and left the window wound down so that he could get some air.

There was a hedge bordering the garden on both sides, and shrubs that threw shadows across the path, giving an eerie feel to the place. She started towards the front door and was about to ring the bell when the dark figure of a man lunged towards her out of the darkness and she came to an abrupt halt, her pulse jerking wildly.

He snarled at her, 'What are you doing here? Come to interfere, have you? We don't need you.'

She recognised Kevin Fraser's surly, slurred voice, and panic rose in her throat as he swung at her, grabbing her by the arm.

'I was called to the house to see your wife. I have to make sure she's all right.'

'No, you don't.'

'I do, Mr Fraser. Will you please let go of my arm?'

'I told you, we don't need no interference.' He threw

her back against the wall of the porch and as she cried out he hit her across the face.

Her head banged against the wooden doorframe, and her senses reeled for a minute. He seemed to tower over her, a huge black form, his face inches away from her own so that she could smell the alcohol on his breath. His large hand gripped her throat, making her choke.

As he moved in closer she felt as though she was suffocating. Fear welled up inside her. She was back on the demolition site, trapped by black shadows and snarling teeth, and she couldn't see, she couldn't breathe, she felt as though she was going to be sick. Then a shudder racked her body and something in her rebelled against the sense of helplessness. She felt anger growing inside her, a burning, deep-seated anger that she should be reduced to a quivering wreck by this man. What right did he have to do this to her?

The feeling of rage built up and gave her the strength to fight back. She stamped down hard on his foot and then aimed a sharp kick at his shin. It was enough to take him unawares and make him stumble for a second or two, long enough for her to press her advantage and shove him back hard with all the force she could muster.

He staggered backwards and fell, and then she saw Toby leap from the car and bound towards them. His lips were curling back, and his teeth showed sharp and menacing, and he was growling—a harsh, savage threat that made Kevin Fraser's face freeze in shock. Toby pinned him to the ground and Heather waited a moment until she saw that it was a threat and only that. Toby wasn't going to take a chunk out of Kevin Fraser unless he made a move and, from the looks of things, Kevin realised it too.

She picked up the medical bag, which she had

dropped, and banged on the door, breathing hard and trying to keep a hold on her self-control.

Natalie was already at the door, pulling it open. 'I thought I heard— Oh, my, are you all right?' She looked beyond Heather towards the garden and gave a shocked gasp, then recovered herself and said, 'Mum's in the living room. She's lying down. Every time she gets up she goes dizzy and can't breathe.'

'I'll go and see to her. Keep an eye on your father— from a distance.'

Heather went through to the living room and spoke to Mrs Fraser, who had a bruise beneath one eye and was nursing her arm.

'I can't get my breath...' the woman said hoarsely. 'Tight band...round my chest.'

Heather examined her, then opened her bag, took out a bottle of tablets and shook one into her hand.

'Swallow this,' she said, reaching for the glass of water that stood on a low table by the settee. She helped Mrs Fraser to hold the tumbler and drink, then persuaded her to lie down again.

'I don't think your injuries are anything to worry about,' she murmured after a while, 'but you're having a panic attack and you need to be calm. Just lie still for a bit longer and it will pass. I'll give you something to tide you over the next couple of weeks, then you can come to the surgery and we'll check up on you again.'

As she said it, it occurred to her that she probably wouldn't be there by then, but the thought swamped her with an unexpected feeling of sadness and she pushed it to the back of her mind.

Natalie came into the room after a few minutes, looking pale-faced and concerned. 'Is she going to be all right?'

Heather explained that she was, and Natalie said

fiercely, 'You should leave him, you know, Mum. Look what you're putting yourself through. Come and stay with me for tonight. I'll look after you. We'll sort out what's to be done in the morning.'

Her mother sat up slowly. 'Would you mind? I don't want to stay here just now. Perhaps I...' She hesitated and then went on, 'I'll spend some time with my sister after that, and think things through. He's not going to change, is he?'

Natalie shook her head. 'Not without a lot of help, and he's got to realise that he needs it first. Come on, let's get you away from here. I rang Mick. He'll be here with the car any minute now. We've time to get a few of your things.'

Heather prepared to leave as she helped her mother upstairs. 'I'll leave a prescription for her,' she said, when Natalie came back down a moment later. 'The tablets will stave off the worst effects of the attacks.'

'Thanks.' She looked at Heather and said awkwardly, 'I'm sorry for what my dad did to you. You'll have a nasty bruise on your cheek tomorrow.'

'Don't worry about it,' Heather said. 'How are you feeling, Natalie? Did you go for your scan?'

The girl smiled. 'Everything's fine this time. Mum says we're going to have to start planning a wedding before I get too big.'

'Is that what you want?'

'Yes, I think so. We'll be a proper family that way. I want everything to be right for this baby.' She glanced up the stairs. 'I'd better go and give Mum a hand.'

'I'll see myself out,' Heather said. 'Will you manage, with your father out there?'

'Mick will be here soon. He'll take care of things.'

Heather went out to the front of the house, steeling herself to deal with Kevin Fraser until Mick arrived.

There was the option of ringing the police, she supposed, but the two women seemed to prefer to handle things themselves.

She stepped onto the porch and saw that Kevin Fraser was no longer alone. Her heart gave a kind of jump when she saw who was there with him. The tall, powerful figure was heart-warmingly familiar. 'Ross...'

Ross let go of Kevin's collar and pushed him away, and another man stepped out of the shadows. Mick? Probably. She left him to deal with Kevin Fraser and feasted her eyes instead on Ross, who had started along the path towards her. She realised that she was shaking. All the events of the last hour were beginning to catch up with her.

'Heather, there you are, thank heaven... What's happened to you? Your poor face...' He stroked her cheek gently with his thumb and drew her towards him, holding her close as though he would take all the hurt away. 'You should never have come here. I told you—'

'You're not going to lecture me now, are you?' she said in a choked, rueful voice. 'I don't think I—'

He shook his head, his mouth tilting in a wry grimace that almost made her smile except that she was feeling too trembly to do much of anything just then.

'What did he do to you?' he asked.

She explained what had happened, and how Toby had come to her rescue.

His mouth set in a grim line. 'I guessed that was about it. I thought something like this might happen, and then when I saw Fraser and Toby—you can't imagine what went through my mind.' He looked at her, searching her face, and said huskily, 'My poor sweet, I hate to see you hurting.' He turned her towards the car and led her down the path. 'I wanted to keep you safe, but it seems I can't let you out of my sight for a minute.'

'I did all right, though,' she said in a wobbly fashion. 'I got the better of him—with Toby's help.' She hesitated, looking around. 'Where is he, by the way?'

'In my car. You'd better keep him with you every second, if this is the way you're going to go on. Why did I have to get mixed up with such an independent woman? It's a nightmare.'

'You can console yourself,' she muttered unsteadily. 'It won't be for much longer.'

His jaw moved, his mouth compressing. They reached his car and he eased her into it, coming around to let himself into the driver's side.

'What about my car?' she said suddenly, wrenching herself around to look back as he started the engine. 'I should—'

'You should sit still and stay calm. I'll arrange for your car to be picked up later. Let's just concentrate on getting you home.'

She was silent for a while. 'I wonder how things will turn out for the Frasers?' she said sombrely. 'She says she's leaving him.'

'It's for the best, don't you agree?' He turned the car onto the lane leading to the cottage.

'I do. Maybe there's hope if he gets counselling. Why do women go for men like that in the first place, I wonder? Do they manage to hide their true selves from the start?'

He shrugged. 'People change. Perhaps things don't turn out the way they expect them to, and life makes them bitter, or they look for solace in the bottom of a glass. Who knows?' He stopped the car in the drive of the cottage and came around to help her out. 'What you should be thinking about is what you're doing with your life.'

She frowned. What had he meant by that exactly?

Toby followed them into the house, and she went to put the kettle on. 'Will you stay a while?' she ventured. 'Have you eaten yet? You've been out—' She clapped a hand to her mouth. 'Louise—the baby. It went out of my head. Is she all right?'

His mouth twitched. 'She's absolutely fine. She had a little boy. Seven pounds. They're both doing well. John's with her now.'

'Oh, I'm so glad for them. I can't think why I didn't ask straight away.'

'I should think you've had more than enough on your mind for the last hour or so.' He took the kettle from her and put it on the worktop. 'Go and sit down. I'll see to that. I want to take a look at the bruise on your face. Were you hurt anywhere else?'

'The back of my head's a bit sore, but I'll survive. There's no need to fuss.'

'There's every need.' He checked her injuries, and seemed satisfied that nothing was too amiss. 'You might have been badly hurt. As it is…' He tugged her to him and dropped a kiss on her brow. 'Come on. Let's go through to the living room and make you comfortable.'

The room was cosy and warm as she had lit a fire earlier, and he dimmed the lighting and sat down beside her on the settee, pulling her close.

'I was worried out of my mind when I read your note and realised where you had gone. I guessed there might be trouble. I didn't know if I would reach you in time. Then when I saw you…'

His hands cupped her face, his thumbs gently brushing her soft skin, and a shuddery sigh rumbled in his chest as he bent towards her and kissed her tenderly.

Heather's mouth softened under his and she kissed him back, measure for measure, wanting it to go on for ever. She ran her hands over his chest, loving the feel

of him, wanting more. He groaned, his hands moving
over her in turn, tracing the curve of her breast and lin-
gering there, and she gave a soft, shaky sigh of satisfaction as he held her close.

His palm rested on her soft flesh, his thumb gliding
over the firm nub of her breast until she moved desperately against him, her body blending with his as though
she would be one with him. Fire was stealing through
her veins and her heart was thundering out of control.
Her whole body pulsed with aching need. It wasn't
enough to feel, to touch—she wanted all of him. She
wanted to be part of him.

He must have sensed her need because somehow they
finished up upstairs, their clothes strewn about the room,
and they were lying on her big bed, their limbs tangling,
a fever of desire in his eyes as he gazed down at her.
He ran his fingers over the smooth silk of her naked
flesh.

'You are so beautiful. If you had known how much I
wanted you, dreamed of you…sweetheart…'

'Ross, I want you, too,' she whispered. 'I don't know
how I've lasted so long without you. These last few
weeks have been so hard to bear… You've been so cold
towards me when all the time I wanted, needed…' Her
voice splintered, and he kissed her again, a fiery trail of
kisses that covered every curve and hollow, his mouth
a delicious torment, stoking the raw need within her.

'Are you sure?' he asked raggedly, his breathing
harsh, uneven.

'I'm sure.' She pulled him down to her and he buried
himself in her softness, thrusting deeply, his eyes dark-
ening with passion, the rhythm of his loving driving
them on in a storm of desperate intensity until the world
they were in exploded in white heat and they floated

slowly back to reality on widening ripples of sweet sensation.

They sank back onto the pillows, exhausted. After what seemed like ages, when she had herself under control once more, she wrapped the duvet around herself and leaned on one elbow, gazing down at him, running her fingers over his chest and watching his breathing slowly return to normal. She wanted to drink in his features, every perfect line of his body, so that she would remember for always...

Was this all there was to be—all she would have to keep in her heart for the years to come—this short, joyous time that they had shared? Was this an end or a beginning? She wasn't sure she could bear it, but what had changed?

He opened his eyes and sat up, rubbing his cheek against hers.

'You look sad,' he murmured. 'Are you having regrets?'

'None.' She meant it. Whatever happened, she would always remember that they had had these moments together.

'Are you still thinking of leaving?' he asked, and said quickly, 'Stay...here, with me. How am I going to get by if you go? I can't bear to think of you coping with all and sundry in the big city. It's bad enough here, but at least it's relatively safe.' He looked at her, his eyes travelling over her face as though he would memorise every part of it. 'Won't you rethink your plans? Won't you think about staying on here?'

Something warm swelled in her heart. 'But I thought—you were so determined to be rid of me—you were trying to find my replacement.'

'I was angry and hurt. After Martyn phoned you were talking about selling up, and you were preparing to go back home and leave all this behind... I don't trust Martyn to take care of you. He's scarcely been around these last few months. If you were mine, I'd never have let you out of my sight for so long.' His fingers cupped her chin. 'Surely you can't go back to him, after this? How can you even think of marrying him?'

'I'm not going back to him,' she said simply. 'It wouldn't have worked. I told him it was all over.'

Ross let out a long, slow breath. 'Thank heaven for that. I was hoping against hope that you would see sense. I wanted to talk to you about it, but you were worried about Sam and after that you seemed so clear about what you were going to do. Even though you were against the idea of marriage, it looked as though you were preparing to go back and take up where you'd left off. Do you still feel that way—that relationships can't work?'

'I've always had doubts about marriage,' she said thoughtfully. 'So many break up, don't they? My parents, James. We saw tonight what happens when things go wrong.'

'That doesn't mean that every couple will go down the same road. For every one that fails, there's one that's a success. You and I—we could make a go of it, I'm sure of that. I love you, Heather—I want you to be my wife. I know I could make you happy if you'll just give me the chance.'

'I don't—'

The bedside phone rang, and he groaned. 'We're not still on call, are we? Can't you ignore it?'

She bit her lip. 'I can't do that. What if it's James in trouble, or someone who needs help?'

Grimacing, she picked up the receiver, and shot Ross a glance when she realised who was on the other end. 'It's my father,' she mouthed to him, then spoke into the phone. 'Is something wrong, Dad?'

'I'll say there's something wrong,' her father said tersely. 'It's James. He's taken it into his head to take his family off on holiday when he knows full well I need him here. I want you to call him up. Talk some sense into him. He knows this is a bad time. I need him here to organise things. Of all the insubordinate, irresponsible—'

Ross lifted a brow, and slid an arm around Heather's shoulders.

She waited for the tirade to die down, then said succinctly, 'No, I won't talk to him. He's doing the right thing, in my opinion. He has to concentrate on what's important right now…and that's his wife and family. If you had an ounce of feeling you'd give him your blessing. He's worked hard for years, slogging his way to the top, and for what? To win your approval. It's about time he saw sense. Neither of us has had a chance up to now, where you're concerned, because all you ever see is what's important to you.'

It was the wrong thing to say. 'I've always done my best for you,' her father blustered angrily.

'No, you haven't,' Heather said crisply. 'You've never actually considered what I wanted, or what James wanted. It was always your feelings that mattered. Well, for myself, I gave up trying to get you to understand some time back. I never knew what I'd done to deserve the way you felt about me—until Grandad told me what you thought my mother had done.' She heard a sharp intake of breath on the other end of the line but went on ruthlessly, 'What a waste that was, when you could have been building up a good family life. A pathetic, useless waste.'

'I did care about you,' her father argued. 'I thought Martyn was right for you, didn't I? I thought I was safe-guarding your future, looking after you, and you didn't want to know. You finished with him.' He made it sound as though it was a personal affront.

'I don't need looking after,' she said calmly. 'I can take care of myself. And so can James, it seems, at long last.' She paused, then added, 'There is one thing you can do, though. If you really care so much, you can come and give me away at my wedding. To Ross Kennedy.'

There was a silence at the other end of the line and it was just as well because Ross's arms tightened on her and he kissed her soundly, hugging her to him. When he'd reluctantly freed her lips she went breathlessly back to the phone call, wondering if her father had had a heart attack or something because he was so quiet. Then she heard him begin to laugh.

'What's funny?' she asked.

'Life, I suppose,' he said, and she thought she detected a conciliatory note in his voice. 'You really are my daughter, aren't you? Stubborn...wilful...obstinate. Determined to go your own way.'

'A chip off the old block, you mean?'

The amusement filtered through again. 'That's exactly what I mean.'

She smiled. 'So, are you coming to my wedding?' She looked at Ross and saw his eyes gleam. 'We haven't set a date yet but I expect it will be some time soon. In fact, we were just about to discuss it...'

'I'll be there.'

'Good. And James? What are you going to do about him?'

'What do you suggest I do?'

'Offer him a full partnership. He's earned it. Give him more leave, written into the agreement, otherwise he might suffer a collapse and then you'll be in trouble. He's your right-hand man.'

He chuckled. 'I suppose I'll have to if he's set on having his own way and you won't help.'

He cut the call after a while, and she put her arms around Ross's waist and leaned her head on his chest. He held her tight, then kissed her thoroughly until her limbs went weak.

'What made you change your mind?' he asked eventually, his voice thick and husky.

'I love you,' she said simply. 'And, more than that, we're the best of friends, aren't we? We care about what happens to each other, and together we can overcome all obstacles. I realise that now. I was blinded for a time by all the pitfalls that happen to other people—but you're what makes it different for us. You're strong and steadfast and true and you'll always be there for me, as I will for you.'

'Like Sam and Jenny,' he murmured softly. 'He knew, you know, all along. He was very sure about things even when I had my doubts that you'd ever come to see that I was the right man for you. He said you would keep the cottage and make a deal over the finances with James so that you could watch our children play in the garden and keep the patch of grass worn away under the swing.'

Her eyes sparkled with the sheen of happy tears. 'He was a wise old man. Will you be happy living here in the cottage, do you think?'

'Blissfully happy—as long as you're here too.'

'But what will you do about the accommodation at the surgery?'

'We could extend the facilities at the practice. We've plenty of time to think about that, though. At the moment, all I want to do is to show you how very much I love you…and think about all the children we're going to have…'

'I think that's a wonderful idea,' she told him huskily, lifting her face for his kiss. 'Just heavenly…'

MARGOT DALTON

second thoughts

To Detective Jackie Kaminsky it seemed like a routine
burglary, until she took a second look at the
evidence... The intruder knew his way around
Maribel Lewis's home—yet took nothing.
He *seems* to know Maribel's deepest secret—
and wants payment in blood.

A spellbinding new Kaminsky mystery.

1-55166-421-6
**AVAILABLE IN PAPERBACK
FROM OCTOBER, 1998**

Jennifer
BLAKE

KANE

Down in Louisiana, family comes first.
That's the rule the Benedicts live by.
So when a beautiful redhead starts paying a little
too much attention to Kane Benedict's grandfather,
Kane decides to find out what her *real* motives are.

*"Blake's style is as steamy as a still July night...as overwhelming
hot as Cajun spice."*

—Chicago Times

1-55166-429-1
AVAILABLE IN PAPERBACK
FROM OCTOBER, 1998

MIRA®

EMILIE RICHARDS

THE WAY BACK HOME

As a teenager, Anna Fitzgerald fled an impossible
situation, only to discover that life on the streets was
worse. But she had survived. Now, as a woman,
she lived with the constant threat that the secrets of
her past would eventually destroy her new life.

1-55166-399-6
AVAILABLE IN PAPERBACK
FROM SEPTEMBER, 1998

JASMINE CRESSWELL

THE DAUGHTER

Maggie Slade's been on the run for seven years now.
Seven years of living without a life or a future because
she's a woman with a past. And then she meets Sean
McLeod. Maggie has two choices. She can either run,
or learn to trust again and prove her innocence.

"Romantic suspense at its finest."

—Affaire de Coeur

1-55166-425-9
AVAILABLE IN PAPERBACK
FROM SEPTEMBER, 1998

CHRISTIANE HEGGAN

SUSPICION

Kate Logan's gut instincts told her that neither of her
clients was guilty of murder, and homicide detective
Mitch Calhoon wanted to help her prove it. What neither suspected was how dangerous the truth would be.

*"Christiane Heggan delivers a tale that will leave you
breathless."*

—Literary Times

1-55166-305-8
AVAILABLE IN PAPERBACK
FROM SEPTEMBER, 1998

4 FREE

books and a surprise gift!

We would like to take this opportunity to thank you for reading this Mills & Boon® book by offering you the chance to take FOUR more specially selected titles from the Medical Romance™ series absolutely FREE! We're also making this offer to introduce you to the benefits of the Reader Service™—

- ★ FREE home delivery
- ★ FREE gifts and competitions
- ★ FREE monthly newsletter
- ★ Books available before they're in the shops
- ★ Exclusive Reader Service discounts

Accepting these FREE books and gift places you under no obligation to buy, you may cancel at any time, even after receiving your free shipment. Simply complete your details below and return the entire page to the address below. *You don't even need a stamp!*

YES! Please send me 4 free Medical Romance books and a surprise gift. I understand that unless you hear from me, I will receive 4 superb new titles every month for just £2.30 each, postage and packing free. I am under no obligation to purchase any books and may cancel my subscription at any time. The free books and gift will be mine to keep in any case.

M8YE

Ms/Mrs/Miss/Mr..................................Initials ....
BLOCK CAPITALS PLEASE

Surname ....

Address ....

....

....Postcode..................................

Send this whole page to:
THE READER SERVICE, FREEPOST, CROYDON, CR9 3WZ
(Eire readers please send coupon to: P.O. BOX 4546, DUBLIN 24.)

DEBBIE MACOMBER

Married in Montana

Needing a safe place for her sons to grow up, Molly
Cogan decided it was time to return home.
Home to Sweetgrass Montana.
Home to her grandfather's ranch.

*"Debbie Macomber's name on a book is a guarantee
of delightful, warm-hearted romance."*
—Jayne Ann Krentz

MIRA®

1-55166-400-3
**AVAILABLE IN PAPERBACK
FROM AUGUST, 1998**